THE WHY & THE YES

or

A Quarantine with a View

PETER ULLIAN

SWAMP ANGEL PRESS

ISBN: 978-1-7352476-0-1

DEDICATION

To my wife, kids, and cats, who make our stay-at-home bearable.

Table of Contents

ACKNOWLEDGMENTS

Those familiar with E.M Forster's *A Room with a View* will recognize the inspiration for this story, as well as the ways in which it veers off into its own territory. Those familiar with L. Frank Baum's *The Wonderful Wizard of Oz* may or may not recognize a few of the elements in the middle section.

PART ONE:
The Bertolini, The Plague Ship, and The Ocean View

As Lucy and Charlotte sat on the hotel veranda and watched the surf gently lapping the shore, Charlotte said, "this was supposed to be our view from our room, you know."

"I know," Lucy conceded, hoping her cousin would soon stop kvetching. "Although probably from a little higher up."

"We should get our money back," Charlotte vented.

"They gave us a bigger room."

"On the wrong side of the hotel!" Charlotte exclaimed.

"It's not on the *wrong* side of the hotel," Lucy said, quietly. "It's just on the *other* side of the hotel."

"The side that doesn't look out at the ocean," Charlotte reminded her.

"Our side looks out at the courtyard," Lucy said. "It's a very nice courtyard."

"It's hardly a match for the ocean, though, is it?" Charlotte insisted.

"It's pretty," Lucy said. "It has pretty flowers in it."

"It could be anywhere in the entire world. It's like looking out onto a place that could be anywhere, instead of only here."

"It has a palm tree or two in it," Lucy said.

"They have palm trees everywhere."

3

"Not everywhere," Lucy said.

"It's no view at all."

Lucy looked at her cousin. A few years older than Lucy, Charlotte, in her mid-twenties, was a loyal and protective cousin, who had been something of an older sister to Lucy when she was growing up. Now, however, Lucy, a recent college graduate attempting to find her way in the world, felt confined and smothered by Charlotte. Why were they on this vacation, together, she wondered? It was a graduation present from her parents, delayed by almost a year, half of which Lucy had spent living in her old room in her childhood home, half of which she'd spent living in a cramped apartment with Charlotte as her roommate, working a barely-paid internship at one of the last independent publishing houses, writing company social media posts and content for a web-site that still used late-twentieth century software, an internship arranged by her mother (of course), an internship that paid next-to-nothing, her living expenses subsidized by that same mother. Why had everyone just assumed that Charlotte would accompany her on this vacation to this admittedly beautiful, seaside Hotel Bertolini? No one had asked her with whom she wanted to vacation. Why hadn't she complained? Why hadn't she just gone on vacation with whomever she wanted?

Of course, Lucy knew the answer. She couldn't have taken her brother, Freddy, because he was away at college, and while Freddy happily would have skipped classes for a week, their mom would have been furious – and furious at Lucy, not at Freddy, since everyone expected her to be the "sensible" one, for some reason, although Lucy didn't think she had ever really been particularly sensible, or at least she had never *felt* that way. She could have taken one of her college or high school girl friends – people whose company she enjoyed a great deal more than Charlotte's – but she knew how much Charlotte would have been hurt if she had done that, and although she found Charlotte tedious, she couldn't stand to see Charlotte hurt. It always made her feel super-guilty.

So, the only other person she could have vacationed with, without raising eyebrows, was her boyfriend, Cecil Weis. And she didn't want to vacation with Cecil. In fact, she wanted very much to spend a little bit of time away from Cecil. Not that she spent all that much time with Cecil, and not that there was anything wrong

4

with Cecil, exactly. It was just that Cecil wasn't very much fun in certain environments, sunny beachy ones prime among them, and the idea of vacationing with him at the beach was not an appealing prospect. She'd either never get to the beach, or leave Cecil alone every day while she went to the beach by herself, and feel guilty about it. Neither scenario was acceptable.

So, that left Charlotte.

And really, Lucy thought, she was just being a big baby. Charlotte was a sweetheart. Charlotte had taken in Lucy as her roommate, she had shown her around the big city, she had taken her to plays and musicals with free or discount ticket she'd obtained from Charlotte's workplace, an artisanal microbrewery where Charlotte worked on the marketing team.

But the flip side was, anytime Lucy wanted to go out with her friends, she had to bring Charlotte along, and while Charlotte was nice and everything, she wasn't part of Lucy's circle of friends, so she was always a third wheel. But she couldn't *not* invite Charlotte. That would be rude.

And what if she ever wanted to bring home a boy? Charlotte thought. Of course, she would never. She was with Cecil, even if she only saw him every other week or so, because Cecil was enrolled in a Ph.D program in a different city writing his dissertation on the philosophy of something or other. So, Charlotte never would have brought home another boy. But what if she wanted to? Charlotte's disapproval would be an unbearable honey-pot block. Sometimes Lucy thought the only thing that kept her and Cecil together was Charlotte's inevitable disapproval if ever they broke up. Charlotte liked Cecil. He was the kind of boy Charlotte approved of for Lucy.

Charlotte looked at her glass of wine. "I don't think this is Pinot Grigio, either," she said. "I think it's Chardonnay."

Lucy looked out at the ocean. "Do you think that's one of the ships?" she said, spying a cruise ship on the horizon.

"One of what ships, Lulu?"

"One of those ships from which they won't let the passengers disembark because they all have the virus? One of those plague ships?"

"Oh, don't call them that!" Charlotte cried. "That sounds practically medieval."

"What should we call them?"

"I don't know. Virus ships?"

"Do you think they'll send them back?" Lucy asked.

"Back where?"

"I don't know. To where the ships originated?"

"The passengers are mostly Americans, I think," Charlotte said. "They're going to have to let them come ashore at some point."

"If we had a room with a view, we could keep a watch," Lucy said excitedly. "And see if it just sits out there, or goes somewhere else."

"Lucy!" Charlotte exclaimed. "That's ghoulish."

Lucy was about to roll her eyes, when a shadow blocked out the sun and she heard a voice booming above her: "We have a view!"

Lucy blinked. The sun was behind the man, so most of what she saw was a glowing halo that shrouded his frizzy hair that sprouted out in all directions from under his hat.

"I said, 'we have a view!'" the man cried, again.

"Give her a little space, Dad," said another voice.

An arm gently pulled the booming voice out of the sun and to the side, so Lucy could get a better look.

The booming-voiced man looked to Lucy like a cross between Bernie Sanders and Walter Winchell. He wore a vest, shirtsleeves rolled up to his elbows, and a fedora cocked back on his head, from beneath which wild silver hair sprouted in all directions . His fingers and teeth were nicotine-stained. His vest and shirt were also stained, but with ink.

Next to him stood a rather tall and attractive young man, a few years older than Lucy, perhaps, neatly dressed in a clean short-sleeve button-down and tan shorts. His light brown hair was swept back from his forehead. He had a long, strong nose.

"What my father means to say -- " the young man began.

"We have a view, for Christ sake!" the older man boomed.

"We have a view," the younger man confirmed.

"Well, I'm sure it's quite lovely," Charlotte said.

"It is, actually," the young man said.

"Why don't you take it?" the older man cried, almost shouting.

"Take what?" Charlotte said. She looked aghast, pale as a ghost.

"The view?" Lucy asked, perplexed.

"The room!" the man boomed. "Take the blessed room!"

6

"And the view," the young man said, gently.

"Why don't you take it?" the man asked. He seemed perplexed.

"Well, thank you, but – " Lucy began.

"We couldn't," Charlotte interrupted. "We couldn't ask you to do that."

"You're not asking!" the man said. "I'm offering! George!" He turned to the younger man. "Tell them to take the damn room!"

"It's so plainly obvious that they should," George said, "that I really don't know what else to say."

"I'm sorry, we have to go," said Charlotte, rising to her feet and pulling Lucy out of her chair.

"Why can't we take their room?" Lucy whispered, but not very softly.

"The young lady is correct, why can't you, indeed?" the man bellowed. "That's what I want to know!"

The young man pulled gently on his father's arm. "Ok, Dad, let them think it over."

"What's to think over?" the older man shouted as George dragged him away. "Take the Goddamned room, already!"

Charlotte and Lucy stared at them as George dragged the older man way.

Charlotte was aghast.

Lucy was astonished.

"What the hell do you think that was all about?" Lucy said.

"Con-men," Charlotte said. "Gonifs. Grifters."

"Drifters?" Lucy said.

"Grifters," Charlotte said. "Much, much worse than drifters."

Lucy shrugged. "I thought they were nice."

Lucy and Charlotte retreated to what appeared to be the relative quiet of the courtyard. They sat on a bench by one of the aforementioned palms, and tried to debrief.

"Why couldn't we take their room, again?" Lucy asked.

"Lulu," Charlotte said, appalled at her cousin's naïveté. "What if they kept a keycard and broke into our room in the middle of the night and held us at gunpoint?"

Lucy furrowed her brow. "To what end?"

Charlotte stared down her nose at Lucy, with such intensity, Lucy looked away. "Lucy Haimowitz, do you really need me to answer that?"

Lucy, ashamed, looked at her feet. "They don't seem like those kind of people," she mumbled.

"Of course they don't seem like those kind of people," Charlotte said. "That's how they take advantage of naïve young girls like you."

Lucy pouted. "I'm not naïve."

"Fine. We're keep our rooms, though."

"Excuse me," said an unfamiliar voice. "Charlotte? Charlotte Badgett?"

Charlotte and Lucy looked up at a serious, studious-looking man of middle age.

"Rabbi Bobe?" Charlotte said.

"Bobe?" Lucy said.

"Call me Artie, please," the Rabbi said.

"Lucy, this is the new Rabbi up by Lake Eden," Charlotte said. "Lucy's family has a weekend place up there, Windy Corners. The Haimowitzes."

"I know your mother, of course," the Rabbi said. "And your brother, Freddy."

"Freddy's sort of a goofball," Lucy admitted, shyly.

"Rabbi, what are you doing here?" Charlotte asked.

"I'm taking a short vacation," Rabbi Bobe said. "The same as you are, I guess."

"I didn't know that Rabbi's went on vacation," said Lucy, mischievously. "Unless it was to study Talmud in Jerusalem or something."

"Well, we never stop thinking deeply spiritual thoughts," the Rabbi said. "But we vacation from time to time. May I?"

The Rabbi gestured to the bench.

"Of course," Charlotte said, as she and Lucy slid over.

"So, how are you enjoying your stay at the Hotel Bertolini so far?" the Rabbi asked.

"They messed up our room," Lucy pouted.

"We were supposed to have a view," Charlotte explained.

"Oh, I'm sorry to hear that," Rabbi Bobe said. "I'd offer you my room, but I haven't got a view, either."

"These two strange people offered to exchange rooms with us," Lucy said. "But Lotte said no."

"Of course I said no," Charlotte said.

"That sounds bold of them," the Rabbi said. "Who were these two people?"

"We don't know their names," Lucy said.

"One was older, with a stained shirt and a vest and a Fedora," said Charlotte.

"He looked like a cross between Bernie Sanders and Walter Winchell," Lucy said.

The Rabbi laughed. "I know exactly who that is."

"You know who Walter Winchell is?" Lucy asked.

"I know who the man is who offered to swap rooms with you," the Rabbi said. "And who Walter Winchell is."

"Who is Walter Winchell, again?" asked Charlotte, quietly.

"Izzy Emison," the Rabbi said.

"Walter Winchell is Izzy Emison?" Charlotte asked.

"Walter Winchell was a radio guy," Lucy said, sharply. "From, like, the 40s. He narrated *The Untouchables*."

"The movie?" asked Charlotte, perplexed.

"The TV show," Lucy explained, impatiently. "From the 60s."

"I thought you said he was from the 40s."

"He didn't die when the 40s ended, Lotte. His radio career was in the 40s. He was like Rush Limbaugh, but less anti-Semitic. Because he was a Jew. He did the narration for *The Untouchables* TV show in the 60s."

"I've never seen it," Charlotte said.

"That's not my fault," Lucy grumbled.

"I'm surprised you have such a vast knowledge of history and popular culture, Ms. Haimowitz," the Rabbi said.

"I had an expensive liberal arts education," Lucy said. "And call me Lucy."

"Call me, Artie."

"Artie, how do you know Mr. Emerson?" Lucy asked.

"*Emison*," Rabbi Artie said. "E-m-i-s-o-n. They are part of our congregation, now. Up at Lake Eden."

"They're Jewish?" Charlotte said, seemingly scandalized.

"Certainly," said Artie

"If you look like Bernie Sanders and Walter Winchell, you're probably Jewish," Lucy snapped.

"Mr. Emison is an old-time newspaper man," Artie said,

"although his attire is, I guess, a little on the effortful side, if you know what I mean? Journalists no longer had the ink-stained vest and fedora look even when he started out."

"They had more the Bernstein and Woodward look?" Lucy asked.

"Exactly," Artie said.

"He was very rude," Charlotte said. "Does he have dementia?"

"No, he just lacks an indoor voice."

"We were outdoors," Charlotte said.

"Lucky for you," Artie said. "If you'd been indoors, he'd have hurt your ear-drums."

"What kind of articles does Mr. Emison write?" Lucy asked.

Artie smiled. "I guess they call it "advocacy journalism." He was a socialist before it was cool."

"Like Bernie Sanders?"

"More like Eugene Debbs. Old time, labor-movement socialist. He was out of fashion the moment he started, and now the fashion has come around back to him again."

"He sounds unbearable," Charlotte said.

"Do you think we should have taken his room?" Lucy said.

"I'm sure it would have been fine," the Rabbi said.

"He wouldn't have broken into the room at night and tied Charlotte up and spanked her with a copy of *Mein Kampf*?" Lucy asked.

Charlotte looked at her cousin, aghast.

"Absolutely not," Artie said.

Lucy turned to Charlotte. "You see, Lotte? We could have had a room with a view."

"I wouldn't have felt right about it," Charlotte said. "What if they leave bedbugs?"

"I promise we'll take the bedbugs with us," said a voice.

Charlotte, Rabbi Bobe, and Lucy turned to see the younger man who, with Mr. Emison, had originally offered the room with the view.

"Ladies, this is George Emison," Rabbi Bobe said. "George, this is Lucy Haimowitz and Charlotte Badgett."

"Ladies, please excuse my dad," George said. "I hope he didn't make you uncomfortable. He can come on a little strong sometimes."

"Does he have dementia?" Charlotte asked.

"Charlotte!" Lucy cried, and slapped her cousin's knee.

George did not appear offended. "He doesn't have dementia," he replied. "But he also doesn't have much in the way of social graces."

"He seems too old to be your father," Lucy said. "Are you sure he's not your grandfather?"

"He was in his fifties when I was born," George said. "Look, the offer still stands. You can have our rooms. We'll take yours."

There was an uneasy pause as George looked expectantly at the women.

"You know, George," Artie said. "Lucy's parents have a weekend place up by Lake Eden."

George practically beamed. "Is that so?" he said. "Then we're neighbors."

"Why are you moving up to Lake Eden, if you don't mind me asking, Mr. Emison?" Charlotte said.

"George, please," said George.

"George," said Charlotte, uncomfortably. "Isn't, I don't know . . . Brooklyn more your style?"

Lucy frowned. "Charlotte, what do you mean by that? Are you being anti-Semitic?"

Charlotte looked scandalized. "Lulu!"

"Brooklyn's not our style," George said. "We're not hipster artisanal picklers, or anything like that."

"Is that what hipsters do these days?" Lucy asked, curiously. "Pickle things?"

"I wouldn't know," George said, thoughtfully. "I'm not a hipster."

"Can't master the ironic beard?" Lucy asked.

George shrugged. "Guilty."

He is nicely clean-shaven, Lucy thought.

"Is that what they're called?" Charlotte blurted out, suddenly perplexed. "Picklers?"

Lucy, George, and Artie looked at Charlotte, quizzically.

Charlotte seemed uncomfortable under their scrutiny. "Briners?" she suggested.

"What the hell are you talking about?" Lucy said.

"I just wondered," Charlotte said defensively. "What you call

11

people who make pickles."

"No one here makes pickles," Lucy said.

"I know that, Lulu," Charlotte said.

"Ok, then, Lotte," Lucy said.

"Lotte?" George said. "Like Lotte Lenya?"

"Exactly!" Lucy cried.

George, to everyone's astonishment, sang a few bars of "Surabaya Johnny" in English, but with a German accent.

He had a pretty good voice, Lucy thought. She decided he was handsome. She was trying to decide if he was interesting.

George finished, and the three of them gave him a polite round of applause.

"Well, it's settled then," George said. "We'll make the exchange as soon as Dad is finished with his bath."

George sauntered away, jauntily.

Charlotte looked poleaxed.

"We'll ask the Bertolini to thoroughly clean the room before you move in," Artie said, reassuringly.

"Especially the tub," Charlotte said.

When they finally took possession of the room – and, they were assured, both sets of key cards – it was immaculately clean, but for a large sheet of paper on the wall with a giant question mark drawn upon it in crayon.

Lucy and Charlotte stared at it for several moments.

"What the hell do you think *that* means?" Charlotte said.

Lucy stared at the question mark, still trying to decide if this George character was interesting.

As Lucy stared at the question mark on the wall, Charlotte went to the minibar.

"They have Pinot Grigio," Charlotte said.

"Pour me a Jameson," Lucy said.

"Lucy," Charlotte admonished. "Don't get drunk."

"Why not?" Lucy said, her eyes still upon the question mark. Why crayon, she wondered? Was he mocking them? Was he being playful? Where did he get the crayon? Did he steal it from a child?

"It's expensive to drink from the minibar," Charlotte said.

"My mom is paying," Lucy said.

"Thanks for the reminder," Charlotte said.

"Is there ice?" Lucy asked.

"There is no ice," Charlotte reported.

"I will be a sweetie and get some, then," Lucy said, picking up the ice bucket.

"I'll do it. I might as well make myself useful," Charlotte said, as she attempted to wrestle away the ice bucket from Lucy. "After all, your mom is giving me a free vacation and everything."

"It's the least Mom can do," Lucy said, trying to be nice. "After all, you've put me up all these months."

"I haven't put you up," Charlotte said. "You pay your share of the rent."

"Well, my mother does," Lucy said, finally wresting away the ice bucket from Charlotte's grip.

As she walked down the hall, Lucy ran into George, who carried a full ice bucket.

"How do you like your view?" he asked.

"I'm sure it's very nice," Lucy said, cautiously. "We haven't really had a chance to enjoy it, yet. We're still settling in."

"Of course," George said, with a smile on the corner of his mouth.

Lucy couldn't decide if she liked his smile. It looked to her like the knowing smile of someone who knew everyone was telling him lies, just as he expected them to.

"The ice machine isn't working down that hall," George said, pointing to the hall down which Lucy was traveling. "You have to go down the other hall. Here, take mine."

"Don't be silly," Lucy said. "You've done quite enough for us, already."

"Here, come on, it's no problem," George said, handing her the full bucket and taking the empty one from her hand.

Lucy looked into the full ice bucket suspiciously.

"It's all there," George assured her.

Lucy looked up at him. "What's all there?"

"The ice," George said. "Every cube."

Lucy frowned. "Did you leave a crayon drawing of a question mark in our room, George?" she asked.

"You know what?" George said. "That's a very good question."

And with that, he turned and walked down the hall the way he had come, softly singing "Surabaya Johnny."

Five minutes later, Charlotte and Lucy sat on their balcony, a Pinot Grigio in Charlotte's hand, a Jameson on the rocks in Lucy's. In front of them, the sun dropped into an ocean shimmering with orange light, as a pelican soared above the surf and a porpoise broke the surface in undulating waves as it swam by.

"Well," Charlotte said. "It really is quite a view."

Lucy was silent for a moment.

"Is that still the plague ship out there?" she said.

Lucy awoke to the most gorgeous pink sunlight she had ever seen streaming through the windows.

She felt rested and energized. She went to the glass doors to the balcony and threw them open. Sunshine streamed in. She felt its soothing warmth envelop her skin.

Lucy walked out onto the balcony and looked down. She saw the hotel veranda below, with a few guests laying out in deck chairs, taking in the morning sun. She looked beyond the veranda and saw the beach, white sand stretching for miles, flanked by dunes and palms. She looked beyond the beach out at the ocean, a shimmering, vibrant eggshell-blue blending into the sky on the horizon, the sun's reflections undulating on its gently rolling surface.

And then she saw the plague ship – if that's what it was – anchored off-shore.

"Lulu," Charlotte mumbled sleepily from her bed. "Get off the balcony. You're in your underthings. People will see you."

"I don't care who sees me!" Lucy exclaimed.

"Your mother would care who sees you," Charlotte said, half into her pillow.

"So, don't tell her!" Lucy said, as she ran back into the room and leaped onto Charlotte's bed.

"Oh, God," Charlotte cried as the mattress bounced. "Don't do that! I've got a headache."

"Are you hungover?" Lucy teased, playfully poking her with a pillow.

"Yes!" Charlotte cried and then, immediately regretting it, said,

14

"Ouch."

"How can you be hung-over and I'm not?" Lucy asked. "You drank wine and I drank whiskey."

"I don't know," Charlotte said.

"Is it because I drank good whiskey and you drank shitty wine?" Lucy suggested.

"How about you go to the dining room and bring us up some coffee?" Charlotte suggested.

"Ok, but I'm going to shower and dress first."

"Why don't you get the coffee first?"

"What if I run into someone we know and I'm all stinky?"

"Whom do we know?"

Lucy counted off on her fingers. "We know the Rabbi, we know Izzy Emison, and we know George Emison."

"We do not know the Emisons."

"We're living in their room!" Lucy cried.

"You're too loud. You're making my head throb."

"Poor Lotte," Lucy said, sympathetically. "Do you have ibuprofen?"

"Just get us some coffee, Ok?"

"Ok, but I might eat bacon first, if they have any."

"Why don't you just bring the bacon up here?"

"Have you ever taken a ride in a hotel elevator with two coffees and a plate of bacon in your hands?" Lucy asked, in high dudgeon.

"Yes," Charlotte croaked. "Many times. For you."

"Well, that was really terrible of me to make you do that," Lucy said. "I will never make you do that again. From now on, I'm a Democratic Socialist, like Izzy Emison."

"He's not a Democratic Socialist," Charlotte reminded her. "He's an old-fashioned labor-movement socialist, like Eugene Debbs."

"What do you want to do today?" Lucy asked. "Go to the beach and take off all our clothes and swim naked in the ocean?"

"Certainly not."

"You're no fun."

"Lulu. Really."

"What then?"

"Get me the coffee, first. Then we'll negotiate."

Lucy showered and dressed in a pair of blue shorts and a light, short-sleeved turquoise blouse. She put on a pair of sensible sneakers, and went down to the dining room and the breakfast buffet. She filled her paper plate with scrambled eggs, bacon, a biscuit, and sausage. She filled a paper cup with coffee and cream, and sat at a table to eat.

As she took her first, reviving sip of coffee, she glanced at the television on the wall, which was tuned to CNN with the sound off but the captions on.

The plague ship was finally being allowed to dock and the passengers to disembark, although they were all being held in a hangar at an Air National Guard base, for a fourteen-day quarantine. Meanwhile, a town in Washington State had reported the first known case of "community transmission" of the virus, whatever that was.

Lucy was about to take a bite of bacon when she heard a voice proclaiming, "do not dare to take a bite of that disgusting swine fat!"

Lucy looked up and saw Eleanor Lavin.

"Miss Lavin!" Lucy cried.

"Miss Haimowitz!" Eleanor cried back.

"I didn't know you were in town."

"Of course I am in town!"

"But what are you doing here?" Lucy said.

"Research!" Eleanor proclaimed. "Life! Are they not, after all, one and the same?"

"I really couldn't say," Lucy admitted.

"My fellow hotel guests!" Eleanor suddenly announced to the other breakfasters in the room. "I am Eleanor Lavin, novelist, and this young, unassuming woman sitting here with her coffee and eggs and bacon, is my twitter voice!" She turned her focus back to Lucy. "I am an author of some modest renown, you may be familiar with my most recent novel, *Love on the Arno*, a semi-autobiographical *Bildungsroman*-slash-*roman-a-cléf* about a young woman's coming of age – spiritually, intellectually, morally, and, yes, I don't deny it – sexually – on a visit to that grandest of Italian cities, *Firenze* – you may know it as Florence – a novel, that I modestly recount to you, made both the *New York Times* and Amazon's bestseller list. Yet, for all my success at letters, I am not a twitterer! I don't do this horrid 'social media.' But this girl – " she pointed to Lucy – "this girl, well, damned if she doesn't capture my voice perfectly in one hundred- and forty-character tweets! God bless this woman! I would not have a social media presence were it not for her diligence and insight! They tell me you can't sell books in this day and age without a social media campaign, and so, I give as much credit to this insightful young woman as I do my own skill with parchment and quill!"

"Does she get a royalty, then?" cried a voice.

It was Mr. Emison, of course. George was nowhere to be seen.

Slightly affronted, Eleanor said, "she receives a salary from the publisher, of course."

"How much do they pay you, Lucy, if you don't mind my asking?" Mr. Emison said. "That's your name, right? Lucy? George was telling me you have pretty eyes! I can see he wasn't lying. Of course, my boy George never lies! Your eyes are damn pretty!"

"My name is Lucy," Lucy said, shyly. She was deeply embarrassed. "Thank you for the compliment, Mr. Emison. And thank you for the room swap, as well. I really do appreciate the view."

Does George really think she has pretty eyes, she wondered?

"And how much are they paying you to make Ms. Lavin's book a success?" Emison shouted. He was sitting across the breakfast room, so this conversation was anything but intimate.

"She didn't make my book a success," Eleanor said, haughtily. "*I* made my book a success. By writing it."

"But she helped sell it, right?" Emison shouted.

"I just said she did."

"And she did her job pretty damn successfully, according to your own account."

"Indeed she did," Eleanor said, with a smile.

"And how much did she get paid for that?"

"That is none of your business, sir," Eleanor said.

Mr. Emison, turning his attention to Lucy now, said, "how much did you get paid, if you don't mind my asking?"

"She certainly *does* mind you asking," Eleanor said.

"Why is everyone so reticent to say how much they get paid?" Mr. Emison said, to everyone in the room. "Doesn't everyone understand that's how the bosses keep us underpaid? Remember, their profits are your unpaid labor! If we had fair wages in this country, we'd have fewer billionaires and fewer bankruptcies, no doubt about it!"

The other breakfasters were completely at a loss as to how to respond to any of this at 8:41 in the morning.

Eleanor turned her attention back to Lucy. "Do not eat that bacon! We will eat, you and I, together, at a place with food that retains the character of its creator!"

"Ok," Lucy said, timidly. What did that mean? she wondered, imagining food that tasted like perspiration.

Eleanor took her by the arm and lifted her to her feet. "Come with me. Right now. I insist!"

As they started for the door, they heard Mr. Emison shouting after them, "do you really use a quill and parchment? You were joking when you said that, right? I myself use an old manual Clark-Nova typewriter. I swear by it! My son George types it all into a computer. I can't stand the things, but that's the only way to reach people these days. My paper stopped print publication last year. We're online only now. Maybe you've heard of it? *The Worker's Weekly Independent Free Press*? I'm the founder, editor, publisher, chief investigative reporter, and content creator, since its founding in 1975!"

Ten minutes later, Eleanor and Lucy were sitting in a nondescript café, eating *huevos rancheros.*

"Isn't this better than the hotel food?" Eleanor asked.

Lucy admitted that it was pretty good, and didn't taste at all like perspiration, although she secretly thought to herself that she regretted never having had a chance to take a bite out of that stack of bacon.

"Today we will go to the museum," Eleanor announced.

"I'd rather go to the beach," Lucy admitted.

"Nonsense," Eleanor exclaimed. "Museum first, in order to heighten our sensual pleasure and the pleasure of our minds, only then to be followed tomorrow by the pleasure of our own senses."

"Ok," Lucy said, not knowing what else to say.

They walked down a side-street of pink stucco buildings with flower beds offering a cascade of color.

"Do you smell that?" Eleanor Lavin said.

"Do I smell what?" Lucy said.

"Stop," Eleanor said, and they stopped. "Smell."

"What am I smelling?" Lucy asked, perplexed.

"The smell of this place," Eleanor said. "Every place has its own smell."

Lucy closed her eyes and breathed in deeply through her nose.

"I smell flowers," Lucy said.

"Latana, a native perennial," Eleanor explained. "Those are the flowers you see lining the sidewalks. They are beautiful, aromatic, and poisonous if ingested. Beauty and danger all in one. Like life itself!"

"I smell the sea.," Lucy said.

"What does the sea smell like?"

"Like salt?"

"What else?"

"Like the breeze."

"You can't smell the breeze."

"You can smell things carried on the breeze," Lucy pointed out.

"Very good," Eleanor said. She seemed pleased. "What else?"

Lucy considered. "Coconut."

"That's sunscreen. You smell it everywhere around here, even miles from the beach."

"I smell sand and sunshine."

"Sand and sunshine don't have a smell."

"I can smell them all the same," Lucy insisted.

"You must have synesthesia," Eleanor said. "You should be a poet. Like Arthur Rimbaud."

The museum was of a modern design, and contained a world-class collection, but Lucy was mortified when she realized Eleanor was dragging her to an exhibition called "Dances with Death: Art in Times of Pandemic."

"Oh my God, do we have to?" Lucy protested. "It's so depressing."

"It's good for your soul, dear," Eleanor explained. "Bracing."

"Isn't it weird they open this exhibit just when that plague ship is docking?"

"Oh, don't worry about that," Eleanor said. "They say the virus is no worse than the flu."

The flu kills a lot of people every year, Lucy thought, but she kept quiet as they entered the exhibition.

The first painting on the wall opposite the entrance was titled *Tournai Citizens Burying the Dead During the Black Death, 14th Century*. It depicted a cramped scene of people carrying caskets on their backs towards men who were digging graves. Two people were lowering a casket into a grave. The faces on all the people looked sad and worried, Lucy thought.

"Notice how there are fifteen mourners and nine coffins?" Eleanor said. "Almost as many dead as living. The Black Plague wiped out at least a third of Europe. Imagine that. Entire communities, wiped off the map. There were forty fewer inhabited towns in Germany after the plague than before."

"But the virus on the cruise ship isn't as bad as all that, right?" Lucy asked.

"Of course not, dear," Eleanor said. "I already told you."

"I just needed to hear it again."

"Lucy, dear, we have much to worry about in this volatile epoch of ours," Eleanor said. "But the virus is not high upon the list."

The next painting they looked at was titled *The Dance and the Triumph of Death*. It was made up of two panels. The first depicted skeletons leading a line of people dressed in a variety of costumes that indicated their profession or status. The second panel depicted Death itself as a skeleton with a crown upon its skull and arms raised in triumph, as Kings and Popes and other high-status people begged on their knees for mercy, offering jewels and gold in exchange for their lives. Death did not appear remotely interested in their earthly baubles.

"You see?" Eleanor said. "Death comes to us all, regardless of how rich or powerful we are in life."

"You can't take it with you," Lucy said.

"You certainly can't," Eleanor agreed. "You can't take it with you into the next life."

"It sure helps a lot if you've got some while you're still in this life, though, doesn't it?" said a gruff and by now familiar voice.

Eleanor and Lucy turned to see Mr. Emison beside them.

Eleanor looked quite put out.

Lucy, to her surprise, found herself unexpectedly delighted.

"Mr. Emison," Lucy said, with mock concern. "Are you following us?"

Mr. Emison threw back his head and laughed with such vigor and volume that everyone in the gallery turned to look. His mirth was a stark contrast to the hushed reverence the other museum-goers brought to the solemn exhibition.

Finally, Mr. Emison said, "No, no, I'm not stealthy enough to follow anybody undetected, I'm sorry to say. I've got two left feet, don't you know. I'd be falling all over myself. In spite of the hat," he said, pointing to the fedora still cocked on his head, "I'm no gumshoe."

Lucy looked him over. Although he was wearing a different shirt, vest and loosely-knotted tie from the day before, these too were stained with ink, nicotine, and other mysterious substances. A button was missing from his vest as well.

"Come along, Lucy," said Eleanor, taking Lucy by the elbow, and dragging her away.

Mr. Emison, apparently oblivious to Eleanor's disdain or to the awkwardness he had created by inserting himself into their museum viewing, followed.

The next painting was titled *The Triumph of Death*, and it was by Peter Brugal the Elder, from around 1562. It depicted an army of skeletons rampaging through a town, killing everything. There was a skeleton slitting a man's throat; others hacking at people with swords and scythes; piles of bodies; naked men and women fleeing in terror; a white-shrouded body in a casket being dragged by skeletons; a dog eating a corpse; a skeleton standing over what appeared to be a King, in full armor with a crown in his head, sitting wounded and weak, the skeleton mockingly showing him the hour-glass it held in its bony fingers; in the distance, all the trees were dead, fires raged, and ships sank into the sea.

It was quite a gruesome painting, and it made Lucy feel, as some of the kids she had tutored part-time after college would have put it, "some kind of way." Its power seemed to have silenced even Eleanor and Mr. Emison.

They moved in relative silence through the gallery to look at the next few artworks. The first was titled *Doctor Schnabel von Rom*. It was painted by Paulus Furst in 1656. It depicted the doctor dressed in one of those terrifying plague costumes, with the wide-hat and the bird-like beaked mask.

Next, they stood before Arnold Böcklin's *Plague* from 1898. It depicted Death as a thin figure with green, decaying flesh, riding on the back of a winged beast, slashing with a scythe, dead bodies on the street beneath him.

Lucy was surprised when they suddenly found themselves in a section of the exhibit dedicated to art of the Spanish Influenza outbreak of 1918-1919. Edvard Munch stared at them from the wall in two portraits, one titled *Self-Portrait with the Spanish Flu,* the other titled *Self-Portrait After the Spanish Flu.* In the one he painted after, he looked tired and drained, dressed in a suit and tie, his eyes haunted. In the self-portrait of the artist with the flu, he was depicted sitting in a chair with a blanket on his lap, and the features on his face seemed to have almost disappeared, giving him a ghostly appearance.

"Where have I heard this name before?" Mr. Emison said. "Edvard Munch?"

"The *Home Alone* painting," Lucy said, playfully. She didn't feel very playful; the artwork had made her feel gloomy. But she needed a break from it all.

"Which one is that?" Mr. Emison said.

"You know," Lucy said, slapping her hands to either side of her face and dropping open her mouth to feign a silent scream.

"*The Scream!*" Mr. Emison cried. "Yes! Of course!"

The next painting took Lucy's breath from her lungs.

It was titled *The Family*, and it was painted by Egon Schiele in 1918. It depicted a couple, a man and a woman, both nude. The woman sat with a baby at her feet, and the man sat behind her. The man was looking at the viewer, the woman looking sadly at something out of the frame. The baby was looking in the same direction.

Lucy, Ms. Lavin, and Mr. Emison all stared at the painting in silence for several moments. When Eleanor and Mr. Emison moved on to the next painting on the opposite wall, Lucy lingered.

Lucy examined several drawings on the wall nearby, also by Schiele. Three were drawings of the artist Gustav Klimt, titled *Gustav Klimt, on His Deathbed.* Another was titled *Portrait of the Dying Edith Schiele,* although the woman portrayed did not look particularly ill, Lucy thought.

Then Lucy read the informational plaque next to the painting.

Lucy learned that Edith Schiele was the artist's wife. She had died of the Spanish flu in 1918. The painting, *The Family,* was a portrait of the artist, his wife, and their as yet unborn baby. The painting had never been completed. Edith, six months pregnant, had died of the flu, and Egon had died three days later.

Lucy looked back at the painting, now with the understanding that she was staring at the image of a family only days away from their deaths. The baby depicted was still inside of Edith. The image in the painting was the artist's imagining of his future child.

Egon and Edith now looked much more vulnerable in their nakedness.

Suddenly, Lucy heard a sob. It echoed in the gallery. Then she heard another.

She realized the sobs were coming from her.

A moment later, she was standing in front of *The Family* wracked with heaving, inconsolable sobbing. She saw people move away from her, skirt around The *Family* in favor of other paintings in the gallery in order to avoid her. She was deeply embarrassed and ashamed. But she could not stop. The painting blurred as her eyes overflowed with tears.

She heard a voice saying, "Here. I've got a package of tissues."

Lucy looked down and could barely see the tissues held before her. She looked at the bearer of the tissues and, through her blurry vision, could just make out George Emison standing at her side, a concerned expression upon his face.

Without forethought or the exercise of better judgement, Lucy buried her face in George's chest and sobbed harder and louder.

She felt George wrap his arms around her back, strong and comforting. A torrent of tears and wretchedness poured from somewhere deep inside of her and into George's cotton shirt. She was no more capable of stopping the wellspring than she was of considering its prudence. She wept, as she had not wept since she was a child, not even when her father had passed away suddenly when she was fourteen. Those tears had come from a deep, truthful place. These were something else entirely. She felt as if these tears had plucked a chord within her soul she had not even known existed. It seemed to contain all the sorrows in the world, from the very first in creation to all the multitude yet to come. Her emotions had become a tidal wave that washed over her and demolished her defenses.

She had no idea how long she stood there, weeping, George holding her in a tight embrace. It couldn't have been less than five minutes, and probably no more than twenty. She had no sense of time. All there was in the universe was her wretched sobbing. She tried to speak, to explain herself, but she had no words to explain herself; she barely understood these feelings that overwhelmed her, much less was she capable of putting them into words. As it was, those words she did try to articulate were swallowed up by choking sobs, and came across as nothing more than inarticulate blubbering.

At length, her sobbing did subside, and as it did, she remained clutched in George's arms, her face buried in his shirt.

Finally, she said, into his chest through a voice hoarse and constricted, "do you still have those tissues, by any chance?"

George handed her the tissues, and Lucy quickly blew her nose, wiped her face, and attempted to dry her tears.

"I'm so sorry," she mumbled.

"Don't be," George said.

"I don't know what came over me."

"You shouldn't be ashamed. You were moved by the art; you were moved by the painting; you were moved by the story behind the painting; you were moved by the depth of human suffering depicted in the painting. Don't be ashamed of that. It's the most natural thing in the world."

Feeling somewhat recovered, Lucy said, "I'm afraid I've left a very large spot of wetness on your shirt."

"It'll dry," George said.

"I'm afraid my nose has run all over your shirt as well," Lucy said, feeling now somewhat more mortified by her snot than by her tears.

"I don't mind," George said, kindly.

Lucy attempted to daub his shirt with the tissue. "I'm really very sorry about this. I don't even know you."

"I'm George," said George.

Lucy smiled. "Hello, George," she said, and she really did feel as if she were meeting him for the first time. "George, your father tells me you never lie. Is that true?"

George looked at her seriously. "I try not to," he said.

"Then I need you to be completely honest with me right now, Ok?"

"Ok," he said, not without trepidation.

"Do I have snot on my face?"

George smiled. "Only a little," he said.

"Oh, God," Lucy said, and tried to wipe her face again.

"Let me," George said, gently taking the tissues form her hands and wiping her face with them.

Lucy should have been mortified to have an almost-stranger wipe snot from her face, but she instead felt somehow cared for, and, somehow, that made it all right.

"Let me walk you back to the hotel," George said.

"Thanks so much, but, really, I'm Ok now," Lucy protested.

"But you're not," George said, grimly. "You need to lie down after a cry like that. You might get light-headed otherwise."

Lucy attempted a wry smile. "Is that your medical opinion, Dr. Emison?" she said.

George did not seem amused, but, at least, Lucy thought, he did not appear offended. "I know a little something about what it is to be inconsolable," he said.

"I'm not inconsolable," Lucy said. Then, warmly, she added, "because you consoled me. That was very nice of you. Thank you for doing that."

"You don't need to thank me," George said. "That's what humans do for each other."

Lucy raised an eyebrow. "To which humans are you referring?" she said. "Because I'm not sure they all would do that."

George just smiled knowingly, took her arm, and guided her out of the museum.

Out on the street, Lucy took in the smells, as she had with Eleanor. She still smelled flowers and coconut; she also smelled lunch. There was a food truck nearby selling fish tacos. Lucy discovered she didn't have much of an appetite.

The sky was an egg-shell blue, and the fresh air combined with the sunshine did indeed make Lucy feel lightheaded. She leaned on George for support.

"How will Eleanor know where I've gone?" Lucy asked.

"I'll text my dad," George said. "He can tell her."

As George texted, Lucy's attention was drawn to a man standing some twelve feet or so away, who was swaying on his feet unsteadily. Beads of perspiration dotted his balding head. His face was flushed.

He began to cough.

The coughing became rather fierce. A dry, barking cough.

After each cough, the man gasped for breath. But each time, the cough came again, and stopped his breath as soon as it had begun.

The man sat down suddenly on the curb and, slowly, tried to take air into his lungs.

He hadn't gotten very far when the coughing returned.

Lucy, without thinking any more than when she had buried her face in George's chest, started towards the stricken man.

George's hand grasped her arm. Where before he had been gentle, now his grip was anything but.

"George," Lucy said. "You're hurting me."

George looked horrified. He loosened but did not relinquish his grip. "I'm sorry," he said. "But don't go near that man."

"George," Lucy said. "That man needs help."

"Not from us," George said, urgently.

"George," Lucy said. "This is what humans do for each other."

George looked worriedly at the man, gasping on the curb. "He has the virus, Lucy."

Lucy looked at the man again, this time with equal parts concern and fear.

"The virus from the ships?" she said.

"It's not getting here only on cruise ships," George said.

"But isn't it just like the flu?"

"It's much worse than the flu. We have to stay away from him. Come with me. I'll take you back to the hotel."

Lucy's feeling, which had gone from sorrow to sympathy, now turned towards panic.

George lead her through a swirl of streets and side streets as he spoke to 911 on his cell phone, reporting the stricken man on the steps of the museum; flashes of swaying palms and flower beds in windows dripping with color whooshed past. Somewhere along the way, the sky, which moments before had been blue and clear, grew ominous and opened up. Palm fronds swirled by in eddies of rainwater running in the gutter. The rain lashed Lucy's face. By the time they returned to the hotel, they were soaked.

"You'd better get out of those wet things," George said.

For a moment, Lucy thought he was offering to get her out of them himself, but after a moment, she understood his meaning.

As they rose together, dripping side by side in the elevator, Lucy wondered to herself if she would have taken him up on the offer if that had actually been his intention.

But at her hotel room door, he bid her farewell, and shook her hand warmly, as if she were a new friend from the office.

Lucy found herself a little disappointed.

Lucy went inside and found Charlotte there, quite cross.

"Lucy!" she cried. "Where have you been?"

Lucy quickly tamped down her desire to tell Charlotte about her adventures. She wanted to share her experiences with Charlotte, but she also knew Charlotte, through disapproval or passive-aggression, would find a way to spoil it for her.

"I went to the museum with Eleanor Lavin," Lucy explained, thinking she had better keep it simple. "She's a writer I worked with at the publishing house. She's in town. I met her completely by accident at breakfast."

"I was worried sick about you," Charlotte said. "I tried calling you, but you left your phone in the room."

"So I did," said Lucy, as Charlotte handed her the phone.

"I thought you were abducted!"

"Who would have abducted me?" Lucy asked.

"The news has been all about that virus, the people coming off those ships, and some of them are really very sick, and they're talking about the first identified case of community transmission, which means someone who hasn't been in China or been in contact with anyone who is known to have got it from someone else who was in China and on a cruise ship or anything like that and apparently part of Westchester County is locked down."

Lucy frowned. "You thought I was abducted by the virus?"

"I didn't know what to think! I hadn't had any coffee! Lucy! You were supposed to bring me coffee!"

Oh my God, Lucy thought. She's right. I was.

Lucy had completely forgotten. She'd run off with Eleanor Lavin and not only had she forgotten to get Charlotte's coffee, she'd completely forgotten about Charlotte altogether and left her sitting alone in the hotel.

Lucy didn't know what to say.

Neither, it seemed, did Charlotte.

"You'd better get out of those wet things, and take a hot bath," Charlotte said.

Soaking in the tub, Lucy thought to herself that she was definitely going to the beach tomorrow, no matter what Eleanor Lavin said.

Later that evening, Lucy and Charlotte shared a room-service meal and ate it on their balcony, overlooking the rain pelting the beach and ocean, and then watched, of all things, Steven Soderbergh's *Contagion* on cable TV. The movie made them both very nervous, Charlotte more than Lucy; Lucy supposed since she had actually seen a person stricken by the virus, she had something solid to wrap her fears around, whereas Charlotte was the victim of TV news and her own imagination.

Lucy waited until Charlotte was in the shower to sneak off and go downstairs.

Off the lobby, she found what she was looking for: an unused banquet room, with a piano.

Lucy found a light switch, went to the piano, pulled off the cover, and ran her fingers over the keys.

The piano was in tune.

Lucy launched into a rendition of "The 1919 Influenza Blues," an old song she'd learned from a collection called *Blues with a Message*. It was a song about the 1918-1919 Spanish Flu epidemic, and how the rich were no more immune than the poor, and the song tied it all into a warning for people to straighten up and fly right, or God would make sure they got the flu, too.

It seemed an appropriate tune under the circumstances.

Lucy was self-aware enough to understand that as an economically privileged Jewish girl, she was not a great messenger for the blues. Accordingly, when she sang the blues, which she did often because she greatly admired the genre for both its form and content, she made no attempt to sing like one of her bluesy singing role models, such as Bessie Smith or Etta James. Instead, she sang like Lucy Haimowitz. She wasn't a great singer, nor a great pianist, she knew, nor a great blues interpreter. But she sang what she sang as well as she could sing it, and she sang it with feeling and with purpose and with honesty. As she sang, she began to feel again the feelings of the day that had undone and overcome her. But the music allowed her to channel those feelings into a form that could, unlike her unmusical self, contain them, and even begin to make sense of them, intuitively if not intellectually. She poured herself, and all of the emotions of the day, into her performance, a performance only for her and the unkempt feelings rattling around inside of her.

Or so she thought.

For, no sooner had she completed her rendition, completing her vocal by breaking into a falsetto as she accompanied herself with a chromatic riff and finishing on the dominant seventh, than she was met with thunderous applause.

She turned to find herself looking at Charlotte, George and Izzy Emison, Eleanor Lavin, Rabbi Bobe, and three people she didn't know: a minister with a white collar and two elderly women.

"Now, that's the thing, isn't it?" Mr. Izzy Emison said, enthusiastically. "I knew you were a young woman of deep feeling, deep and true! Didn't I say as much, George?"

"You did, Dad," George said.

"Was I right?"

"You were right?"

"Do you see?"

"I already knew," George said, sharing a secret nod with Lucy.

Over the course of the next few minutes, everyone congratulated Lucy on her performance, and then, all of a sudden, Lucy found herself alone with the Reverend and the two older women. Everyone had filed out to the bar to continue their conversation. Lucy had every intention of joining them, but finding herself alone with the trio, knew that she had to go through the ritual of small talk.

Lucy, her head swimming with embarrassment at having been caught doing something that she had thought she was doing in private, despite the acclaim her performance had received, attempted to be polite. "I don't think I caught your names," she said.

"I am the Reverend Eager," said the Reverend. "I'm acquainted with Rabbi Bobe from a conference last year in Jerusalem, on the commonalities of the Abrahamic faiths. These are the Miss Alans, who are with our church group. We are on a retreat in this lovely climate, a community-building and spiritual retreat. Unfortunately, we have very little time for sight-seeing or enjoying the weather, such is our schedule."

"Your performance was lovely, dear," said one of the Miss Alans. "You reminded me of Barbara Streisand."

"You're only saying that because the young girl is Jewish, Teresa," said the other Miss Alan. "Her performance, as magnificent as it was, was nothing like Barbra Streisand."

"If you are accusing me of anti-Semitic bigotry, Catharine," said Teresa Alan, "I take great exception. I would remind you that it was *me* who suggested to *you* we see *Annie Hall* instead of *Star Wars* on that balmy spring day in 1977."

The fact that both these women immediately knew she was Jewish made Lucy self-conscious about her nose. Although perhaps, she thought, it was the association with the Rabbi that had given her away. Either way, she was flattered by the comparison to Barbra Streisand, whom Lucy found exceptionally beautiful in movies such as *Funny Girl* and *The Owl and the Pussycat*, and, especially, *Yentl*.

"Since we are on the subject of anti-Semitism, might *I* remind *you*, dear Teresa, that it was *me* who suggested to *you* we see *Manhattan* instead of *Alien* in the spring of 1979," said Miss Catherine Alan.

"I've always resented you for that, Catherine," said Miss Teresa Alan. "I would so love to have seen *Alien* in 1979 before we saw *Aliens* in 1986."

"We saw *Alien*!" Catherine protested.

"On VHS!" cried Teresa. "Not on the big screen. It's not the same thing."

"Well, in any event, it is absolutely great to meet you," Lucy said, hoping to steer the conversation in another direction.

"And how do you know the Emisons, if you don't mind my

asking?" Reverend Eager asked.

"We traded rooms with them," Lucy recounted, brightly. "And then we saw them at the museum."

"They are a very peculiar people," said Miss Catherine Alan.

"That's just your snobbery showing, again," said Miss Teresa Alan.

"That's quite enough of that, if you don't mind, Teresa," said Catherine. "I'll remind you it was I who suggested we see *On the Waterfront* at the cinema in 1954, instead of *Magnificent Obsession*."

"You forget, dear sister, that it was I who dragged you to see *Matewan* instead of *The Big Easy* that weekend in 1987," replied Teresa.

"They are strange people, it's true, I hate to say it," said the Reverend. "The Emisons, I mean."

"What's strange about them?" Lucy asked, although of course she had thought the same thing about them twenty-four hours ago.

"Well, of course, the father's a socialist," the Reverend said.

"But that's quite normal these days," Lucy protested. She suddenly found herself filled with an urgent desire to defend the Emisons.

"The people of Eastern Europe, Cambodia, and Cuba would be mystified that socialism has somehow become fashionable," the Reverend said. "Since it failed them so miserably."

"It's done quite well for the National Health Service in England, though," Lucy countered.

"The N.I.H is an utter failure, Miss," said Eager.

"No it isn't," Lucy said. "The English have longer lifespans and lower child mortality than we do in America."

"They have worse outcomes for cancer treatment," the Reverend said.

"That's true, but fewer English people get cancer in the first place than we do over here," Lucy said.

"Do you remember that time we were in London and I sprained my ankle, Teresa?" said Catherine.

"I do, Catherine," Teresa said. "The N.I.H took very good care of you, if I recall."

"They did indeed. They even gave me tea."

"Tea is no substitute for good medical treatment," the Reverend admonished.

31

"We got that, too," Teresa said.

"Either way, Mr. Emison is no Joseph Stalin," Lucy said.

"But he did kill his wife," the Reverend said.

Lucy was shocked. "Reverend Eager, what do you mean?"

"I have it on good authority," Eager said. "But I can say no more."

"You certainly will say more," Lucy demanded. "You can't just slander a person like that and not back it up."

"I didn't know I was under interrogation," said the Reverend, trying to brush off Lucy's intensifying ire, "but it is no slander. I have it on good authority."

"Whose authority?" Lucy said.

"I'm not at liberty," the Reverend demurred.

"Oh, Reverend Eager, you really are very naughty," Catherine Alan said, "to say such things and just leave us hanging here."

"Yes," Teresa Alan agreed, "there is no point to gossip if you cannot tell us all you know."

"This is not gossip, my good Miss Alans," said the Reverend. "This is established fact."

"Which you're not at liberty to establish for us?" Lucy said, allowing her incredulity to drip from every word. "That's not very well established."

"You'll have to take my word for it," the Reverend said.

"But I've just met you," Lucy pointed out. "And I've met the Emisons two or three times, at least. So, really, I know them much better than I know you, and with all due respect, I don't have any reason to accept your unsupported assertions over the evidence of my own eyes."

"Oh, I like this young woman, don't you, Catherine?" said Teresa.

"Very much," said Teresa. "She's feisty."

"And what evidence is that, if I may ask?" the Reverend said.

"You may ask, because, unlike you, I have no problem divulging my sources," Lucy said.

"But your sources are your own observations, dear," one of the Miss Alans pointed out; Lucy did not see which one.

"Yes, that's true," Lucy admitted. "My own observations, my thoughtful insight, and the intuition of my own heart."

"Oh, Reverend Eager, you have now entered the realm of a

young woman's heart," Catherine said.

"Do tread carefully," Teresa said. "We implore you."

The Reverend shrugged, playfully. "I may be out of my depth," he admitted.

"I should say you are, because you don't know them," Lucy said. "I went to the museum with Mr. Emison the elder."

"Does he have good taste in art?" the Reverend asked.

"I wouldn't say that," Lucy admitted. "But when Ms. Lavin and I were both overwhelmed into hushed silence by the power of the images in front of our eyes, so was he. So, he must be a person of deep feeling, can't you see that? And George saved me from a person with the virus to whom I was heedlessly approaching."

"Which virus?" Catherine said.

"The one from the cruise ships," Lucy said.

"Oh!" Teresa exclaimed. "That one!"

"It's no worse than the flu," Eager said.

"Do you get your flu shot every year?" Lucy asked.

"I do," Eager admitted.

"Well, they don't have a shot for this one," Lucy said. "Besides, George says it's much worse than the flu."

"Is George a medical doctor?"

Lucy paused for a moment. "I'm not actually sure what he does," Lucy admitted.

"Perhaps you don't know him as well as you think?" Eager said.

"I know him well enough to know he didn't hesitate to wipe the snot from my face!" Lucy cried, and immediately regretted it.

There was a pause in the conversation. Her confession seemed to have silenced Reverend Eager.

"Had you been crying, dear?" Catherine Alan asked.

"Yes," Lucy admitted, quietly.

"And young George wiped the snot from your face?" Teresa asked.

"Yes. He did," Lucy said. She could feel her face burning with embarrassment.

"Well, that is an act of love, then," Catherine said.

"We're not romantic," Lucy mumbled.

"She means it was an act of love towards a fellow human," Teresa said.

"But why were you crying, dear?" Catherine asked.

Lucy hesitated. She felt emotion welling in her chest at the memory of it. She tried to speak, and discovered her throat had tighten up and she could barely get the words out.

"The painting," she said at length, her voice cracking.

"It moved you, dear?" said Teresa, gently.

Unable to speak, Lucy nodded, wiping way a tear from her eyes, which were now brimming with them.

"Well, my dear," Catherine said, handing her tissues. "I don't know if Mr. Emison is a man of deep feeling. But I think it's clear that you certainly are."

The next morning, Ms. Lavin lead the way to the beach.

Charlotte and Lucy followed Ms. Lavin, who traversed a trail through the dunes, and then suddenly veered away from the sign that pointed to the beach. Ms. Lavin lead them through more palm-shaded trails until, at length, white sand, blue sky, and rolling surf opened up in front of them. They trudged across the sand towards the ocean until Ms. Lavin announced they had found the perfect spot, where they lay down their towels and beach bags, and set up their beach umbrella.

"Um, Ms. Lavin?" Charlotte said, suddenly sounding quite alarmed.

"Yes dear," Ms. Lavin replied.

"I think everyone is naked on this beach," Charlotte said.

"Of course they are, dear," Ms. Lavin said, as she began to undress. "And soon will we all."

Lucy looked at Charlotte. Charlotte looked mortified. Lucy thought that was hilarious. She began to undress as well.

"Lucy!" Charlotte cried, *sotto voce*. "You're not, are you?"

"Of course I am," Lucy said. "Why shouldn't I?"

"Because everyone will see you!" Charlotte whispered.

Lucy shrugged. "I can see them just as well."

"But, Lucy . . . I could never."

"Why not? We used to skinny-dip at Lake Eden, clad in nothing but that which Hashem gave us," Lucy pointed out, she thought quite sensibly.

"That was when we were kids," Charlotte said.

Lucy thought about it. She supposed it had been some years since Charlotte had joined her and Freddy in the waters of Lake

Eden.

"Well, Freddy and I still do," Lucy said.

"Together?" Charlotte said in horror.

"Of course," Lucy said. "Sometimes with our friends, too. Every summer and most weekends, weather permitting."

"But . . . he's your brother," Charlotte whispered.

Lucy furrowed her brow. "I know he's my brother. Did you think I forgot?"

"But he's nineteen!"

"I remember when he was born," Lucy said. "I was four."

"But isn't that . . ."

"Isn't that what?"

"Weird?" Charlotte asked

"What's weird about it?"

"He's your *brother*."

"We're swimming," Lucy said. "What's weird about swimming? What do you *think* we're doing?"

"Nothing, it's just . . . aren't you embarrassed?"

"Embarrassed about what?"

"To see your brother . . . and to be seen by him . . . you know . . ." Charlotte whispered, like it hurt her soul to say the word: "*naked*."

Lucy looked at her cousin, appalled. "Charlotte. What are on earth do you think goes on when Freddy and I go swimming? For God's sake, Charlotte. What kind of an imagination have you got?"

It occurred to Lucy that Charlotte really had very little idea how being a human actually works.

Lucy and Ms. Lavin by now both stood quite naked. Ms. Lavin was applying sunscreen to herself.

Charlotte looked at Ms. Lavin, quickly looked away at her cousin, and then quickly looked away again.

Lucy realized how strange it was that even though they were roommates, she had never seen Charlotte naked, nor Charlotte her, since they were both children. Charlotte always took care to dress in her room and to exit the bathroom wrapped in a towel or robe. Lucy, without even thinking about it, had done the same . . . perhaps unconsciously recognizing that to do otherwise would discomfort her cousin.

Now Charlotte was standing there, her face reddened in

embarrassment, her eyes glancing uncomfortably at Lucy's nakedness, then darting away.

"You should try it," Lucy said. "I think it might make you happy."

"Why would it make me happy?" Charlotte asked.

"I don't know. It just makes people happy." Lucy gestured at the sunbathers on the beach. "It makes all of these people happy."

"I don't think it would make me happy," Charlotte said.

"You never know until you try it," Lucy said. "You're not very happy with your clothes on, after all. Maybe you'd be happier if you were out of them."

"I'm not unhappy," Charlotte frowned, unhappily. "What makes you say that?"

"It's a scientific fact that being naked in an appropriate social setting with other naked people increases a sense of well-being and confidence, promotes greater life-satisfaction, and fosters higher self-esteem," Ms. Lavin said. Lucy was grateful for the interruption. She didn't want to have to explain to Charlotte why her cousin so often seemed unhappy. "This is firmly established in a study published in the *Journal of Happiness*."

"There's a scientific journal of happiness?" Charlotte asked, incredulously.

"Certainly," Ms. Lavin said. "There's a scientific journal for everything."

Charlotte still did not look convinced.

"Apply to my back and shoulders, would you?" Ms. Lavin said, handing Lucy a tube of sunscreen. "And use it on yourself. Apply liberally. Helios is your friend, but only if you treat him with the respect he deserves."

Lucy took the tube, squirted sunscreen into her palms, then handed the tube to Charlotte.

Lucy applied the sunscreen to Ms. Lavin's shoulders and back, while Charlotte uncomfortably applied it to Lucy's. Then Lucy diligently covered the rest of herself in sunscreen.

"Well, will you look at that?' Ms. Lavin suddenly said. "It's the Miss Alans."

Lucy and Charlotte looked.

Distantly, they saw two rather tall and rather naked elderly women who could well have been the Miss Alans.

"I must go talk to them," Ms. Lavin said. She turned back to Lucy. She looked her up and down with a judicious eye. She walked around Lucy in a circle, examining her. Lucy was not sure what for.

"Excellent," Ms. Lavin said. "You have done an excellent job of ensuring maximum sunscreen coverage to your epidermis. Do not hesitate to re-apply frequently if you want to guarantee you are able to sit down tonight. I can see from your pale, pasty tush that it has been some time since your nether bits have seen the light of day. I was going to invite you to join me to speak to the Miss Alans, but I can see you are quite a healthy young woman, despite your lack of recent sunshine, and you shouldn't wait around for those of us of a certain age – although at sixty, I think of myself in pretty good shape. Even so. Go. Enjoy. Charlotte, get undressed now, quickly, so Lucy can help you apply sunscreen to the hard-to-reach regions. We shall see one another again at the umbrella."

With that, Ms. Lavin began marching purposefully towards the Miss Alans.

"She is in really good shape for a woman of sixty," Charlotte agreed, as they watched her march over the sand.

"Get undressed so I can help you with the sunscreen," Lucy said.

"I'll just stay under the umbrella, thank you," Charlotte said.

"Are you sure?"

"I don't want people looking at me."

"That's not what it's about, you know."

Charlotte looked perplexed. "That's not what *what* is about?"

Lucy raised her hand expansively, indicating the environs and its inhabitants. "This," she said. "It's not about *seeing*. It's about *being*."

Charlotte looked her in the eye for a long time. "I have no idea what that even means."

No. You really don't, thought Charlotte, sadly.

"Well," Lucy said, "go swimming with me and keep your swimsuit on, then."

"Oh, no, I could never," Charlotte said. "I'd be so self-conscious to be the only one on the entire beach wearing a swimsuit. I'll just stay here."

Poor Charlotte, Lucy thought. Too self-conscious to wear a

swimsuit. Too self-conscious not to.

Lucy sighed. Then, without another word, she turned and took off running away from Charlotte and towards the waiting ocean.

The sand was hot, but not too hot. She reached the wet, packed sand, and then her feet were running in the lapping foam of the broken waves as they swirled up that expanse of the beach. She felt the sun already beating down on her shoulders. She began to splash through water up to her ankles, and then she reached the break where small waves came rolling in. She ran into a wave, and water exploded around her; she ran further still, then dove into another.

She was underwater, the water warm as a bath, the roar and swirl of the wave above her; she broke the surface, gulped air, swung her wet hair back over her head. She put her feet down and felt the sandy bottom. Another wave was rolling in. She timed it. She caught the wave and body surfed for about twenty seconds, before she ended up under water, her feet in the air.

She continued to body surf several more waves, only incrementally more successful with each one. Finally, she managed to ride one partly into shore. Afterwards, she knelt in the sand as small waves broke against her back. She scanned the beach and saw Charlotte, now far away. Her body surfing was carrying her progressively further away from her cousin. Lucy didn't much mind.

Lucy got to her feet and walked along the foam where the surf lapped the sand and then drew back. She looked about her. A pelican soared above the waves. She saw, distantly, a porpoise break the surface, a puff of air expelled from its blowhole. Up ahead, a naked family with small kids were building a sandcastle. Naked couples strolled up and down the beach, men and women, woman and women, men and men, holding hands. Most were middle-aged or older; some had clearly spent too much time in the sun, their bodies tanned to a leathery bronze. A younger couple, collegiate, perhaps Freddy's age, walked towards her. The boy was white, the girl Asian.

They were gorgeous.

Lucy watched them as casually as she could manage. As they passed, she feigned interest in a seashell at her feet, so she could stop and watch them walk away.

She rose, her heart slamming in her chest; she didn't quite know why. She was intoxicated by the sensations of the place, the smell of sunscreen, the feel of it and the sun on her shoulders and her nose, the soft embrace of the foaming water at her feet, the breeze in her hair and on her skin. Her breath felt short and she felt giddy.

She came upon a spot where the waves rolled in with sufficient force to offer good body-surfing, yet were gentle enough she thought she could handle them. She waded into the water, kicking it into spray before her, until the water came up to her waist and she dove into a wave and, once upon the other side, wiped the seawater from her face, and body surfed the next one in.

She continued this way for some time, joyfully, until she misjudged the force of a wave and felt a moment of panic as she rode atop it, helplessly, and the wave curled and crashed and she rushed down its curve and was tossed head over heel under the surface. For a moment she felt a panicky fear of drowning, and then finally the wave spat her out on the shore, and she found herself with her face in the sand and her ass in the air.

"That's it!" a voice cried, "That's the way! I knew it, Ms. Haimowitz! I knew you were the kind of person to grab the world by its horns and ride it!"

The voice belonged to the elder Mr. Emison.

Lucy felt she should have been more embarrassed than she was, given the awkwardness of the position she found herself in, face in the sand and tush in the air. But she found she was so relieved to have survived the wave, that she didn't really care about much else.

Lucy peeled her face from the sand, sat upon her knees, as gentle surf foamed around her, and looked up at Izzy Emison, who was wearing nothing but his fedora and possibly sunscreen.

"I saw you ride that wave into shore – magnificent!" Mr. Emison said. "I only wish my son George was here to see it, Ms. Haimowitz!"

Lucy found, to her surprise, that she also wished George had been here to see it. She knew not from where this feeling had come. She pushed it aside, as she wiped the sand from her face.

"Please," she said. "Call me Lucy."

Mr. Emison offered her his hand, and Lucy took it, gratefully. He helped her to her feet. She was impressed by the strength in his arm.

Lucy would have expected herself to feel mortified to have run into Mr. Emison, both of them wearing nothing but seawater and sunshine. To her surprise, she didn't feel awkward at all. The whole thing seemed quite oddly *normal* . . . even a little bit *mundane*.

"Mr. Emison – " she began, before he interrupted her and asked her to call him Izzy. "Izzy," she corrected herself. "I was just taking a walk down the beach," she said, pointing in the direction opposite from which she had come, back where Charlotte, presumably, still waited beneath the beach umbrella. "Would you like to join me?"

"That'd be splendid!" Izzy Emison said.

They began to walk together down the beach.

"I won't walk with you very long," Izzy said. "A young person like you, you shouldn't have to slow down for an old man like me."

"Not at all," Lucy assured him. "I'd enjoy the company."

"Never trust an enterprise that requires the wearing of clothes, that's what I always say!" Izzy declared.

"That seems a useful philosophy," Lucy said.

"I am, Lucy, as I can see you are as well, an adherent of the return to nature movement."

"Is there such a movement?" Lucy asked.

"And well you may ask!" Mr. Emison all but shouted. "Because how can we *return* to nature when we have never been *with* her? We must *discover* nature. The Garden of Eden, which theologians place in the past, is really yet to come. We will enter it when we no longer despise our bodies. In this, I'm afraid, men are ahead. We despise the body less than women do."

Lucy wondered if that were true. Was that why Charlotte refused to join her, and always hid her nakedness? Lucy had assumed she was prudish. But perhaps, she wondered, she was ashamed. This made her feel a little bit sorry for Charlotte, and a little bit guilty about some of the less charitable thoughts she had of her.

But, Charlotte aside, was this true of women in general? Lucy wondered if Izzy Emison's ideas about such things, despite his progressive point of view, were outdated. She certainly knew plenty of men who had very poor body-image.

"But I see you do not despise the body, Lucy," Mr. Emison continued. "You do not despise the body God has given you. Good for you!"

Was that true? Lucy wondered. Did she or did she not despise the body? She knew she did not despise bodies in general. She thought bodies, while occasionally ridiculous, were perfectly customary, and she was not offended by seeing them or being in proximity to them as long as the proprietors of those bodies were behaving in a socially appropriate manner. She suspected Charlotte had been quite traumatized by the exposure of so many bodies this day, and would possibly have been psychologically damaged beyond repair had her own body been unexpectedly revealed to Mr. Emison or any other recent acquaintance. So, Charlotte was clearly very disconsolate about bodies in general, those of friends, family, and recent acquaintances especially, and Charlotte's own in particular.

Lucy knew she did not feel as Charlotte did. But Lucy wasn't entirely sure how she actually did feel. She'd never really given it much thought. She did not think she despised her own body. She'd never thought of herself as a great beauty; she always felt her legs were a little too short, her butt a little too big, and her boobs a little too small. But she was glad she had a body healthy and strong enough to hike, swim, ski, run, play tennis, and walk on the beach. She wasn't ashamed of or embarrassed by it. It worked, it worked well, and, all things considered, it looked Ok. She wasn't quite sure she was proud of it, however. Was that a prerequisite to entering the Garden of the future, as Mr. Emison envisioned it? Or would that be too conceited to feel that way? What did it mean, she wondered, to "not despise" something? Was that enough?

She suddenly found herself, unlike mere moments earlier, feeling self-conscious about her nakedness. Mr. Emison may have been right, on the whole, about Lucy's attitude towards these things, but now that he had brought it up, she felt much too self-aware of her own body for her own comfort. Perhaps, she wondered, talking about not despising one's own body was not entirely conducive to not despising one's own body.

"I knew when I saw you singing and playing the piano that you were a person of unusually deep humanity," Mr. Emison said. "That gives you an advantage. You are the future, Lucy, you and

George, and not just because of your youth. You are the future because you understand that we are all comrades and when we do not despise ourselves, only then can we enter the Garden."

Lucy was confused. "Is this socialism?" she asked. "All this talk about nature and bodies and music and gardens?" She'd studied socialism in school and voted for Bernie Sanders in the primary in 2016 when she was a freshman in college and had just turned eighteen, but she didn't remember this part of it.

"The deepest part of it, Lucy," Mr. Emison said. "The truest part. I know you understand what I'm talking about, in your heart if not in your head, because I can see you live it. George, however, is the opposite. He understands it in his head and tries to live as if he feels it in his heart, but he does not feel it in his heart."

"Oh," Lucy said, perplexed. "I'm sorry to hear that."

"How can he be unhappy when he is strong and alive?" Mr. Emison exclaimed "What more is one to give him? And think how he has been brought up—free from all the superstition and ignorance that lead men to hate one another. With such an education as that, I thought he was bound to grow up happy. What are we to do with him? Here he is, poised like you to enter the Garden, and yet – he is unhappy."

Mr. Emison suddenly stopped walking and turned to face Lucy. Lucy, bewildered, turned to face him as well.

"I would like to ask you to be George's friend," Mr. Emison said.

"I should hope that we are already friends, Mr. Emison," Lucy said.

"Izzy," said Mr. Emison.

"Izzy," Lucy corrected herself.

"I'm asking for a little bit more than that," Mr. Emison said. "I'm asking you to try to understand him."

"Understand him?"

"I'm not asking you to fall in love with him," Mr. Emison clarified. "Just be his friend. You are nearer his age, and the both of you must allow yourselves to pull out from the depths of your being those thoughts that you do not understand, and spread them out in the sunlight and know the meaning of them. By understanding George you may learn to understand yourself. By understanding you, he may learn to understand himself. It will be good for both of you."

To this extraordinary speech Lucy found no answer.

"I only know *what* it is that's wrong with him; not *why* it is," Mr. Emison said, sadly. "He has never been the same since he lost his mother."

Although Lucy did not for a minute believe Mr. Eager's scandalous slander, she could not help but press the matter, now that it had been raised. "How did she die, if you don't mind my asking?"

"The cancer," Mr. Emison said.

That certainly did not sound like murder, Lucy thought. "Then it's grief that makes him this way?" she asked.

"It's worse than grief; things won't fit."

"What things?"

"The things of the universe. It's quite true. They don't. George and I both know this, but why does it distress him so much? We know that we come from the winds, and that we will return to them; that all life is maybe a knot, a tangle, a blemish in the eternal smoothness. But why should this make us unhappy? We should love one another, and work and rejoice. I don't believe in this world's sorrow. And I can see you don't, either."

Lucy didn't think she did, and she said so. She had felt the world's sorrow yesterday in the museum; felt it deeply. But she did not live by it, and did not intend to do so.

"If George could see you now, he would know. He would know that the world, for all its lousy faults, is also filled with beauty, and moments of transcendence. I know you know this, just as I do. Make my boy think like us. Make him realize that by the side of the everlasting *Why* there is a *Yes*—a transitory *Yes* if you like, but a *Yes* nonetheless."

He looked at her, plaintively, with such pleading in his eyes that Lucy, although confused, said, "I will do my best."

Mr. Emison smiled. They resumed their walk along the beach.

In due course, they ran into the Ms. Alans and Ms. Lavin. All three wore nothing but garlands of bluebonnets strung together, in which they were festooned, accented with bluebonnets in their hair. Lucy thought the Miss Alans looked somehow grand in their bluebonnets and unashamedly aged skin.

"Oh, Hello Ms. Lucy," cried Teresa, "Do you see how dear Mr. Emison has picked and strung bluebonnets for us?"

Lucy turned towards her walking companion, impressed.

"You did that?" she said.

Mr. Emison laughed. "With George's help," he said.

Was George around here somewhere? Lucy wondered. The idea made her heart beat faster and gave her butterflies in her tummy. This confused her. She pushed the sensation aside.

"That was very thoughtful of you, Izzy," Lucy said.

"As it turns out," Catherine said, "Mr. Emison and Teresa and I are previously acquainted."

"Is that a fact?" said Lucy.

"We met at Woodstock!" Teresa cried.

Lucy felt her eyes widen. "You guys were at Woodstock?"

"We met all bathing naked in the river with the other hippies," Catherine said.

"I was nineteen," Mr. Emison said, wistfully.

"We were already in our forties," Teresa said. "but we've always lived adventurously."

"Izzy made us a garland of wildflowers then, too, to wear around our necks and in our hair," Catherine said. "He was always so thoughtful."

Lucy was even more certain now that there was no possible way Mr. Emison could have murdered his wife.

"Where is Charlotte?" Ms. Lavin demanded.

"Under the umbrella, I think," Lucy said.

"Re-apply!" Ms. Lavin commanded, as she handed Lucy a tube of sunscreen. Lucy was pretty certain Ms. Lavin had left her own sunscreen at the umbrella, so this, she surmised, must belong to the Ms. Alans.

As she dutifully re-applied, Lucy asked, uncertainly, "is Reverend Eager here?"

The Ms. Alans both laughed.

"This is not the kind of place one finds the good Reverend," Catherine said.

"We snuck away," Teresa admitted.

"I haven't seen the Rabbi, either," Ms. Lavin said.

"We have a perfectly clerical-free day ahead of us!" Mr. Emison declared.

Once the sunscreen was fully re-applied, with assistance from the Ms. Alans and another inspection by Ms. Lavin, Lucy said, "well, I'm going to continue my walk along the beach."

"Look for George, will you?" Mr. Emison said. "Be his friend."

Lucy resolved that she would look for George, and she would be happy if she found him. And she would befriend him, if he were amenable.

Lucy walked along the wet sand, the water lapping her feet. She felt inexplicably wonderful. She felt the sun on her shoulders, the breeze in her hair, the ocean spray upon her skin. It seemed hard to credit dire warnings about killer viruses on plague ships and community transmission and all that. Life was wonderful. The best things in the world were right here and they were absolutely free, if you didn't count the parking fees, and since she could walk here from the Bertolini, she didn't have to park, which was good, because she didn't have a car. The sun shone joyfully and the ocean rolled merrily and warm breezes caressed the body she did not despise ever so lovingly. All around here were people perfectly comfortable in bodies they did not despise. Perhaps the Garden was right here, she thought. Perhaps we entered the Garden every weekend or vacation and did not know it because Monday or the end of vacation always beckoned with its myriad responsibilities.

Lucy stopped walking and looked out at the ocean, her attention drawn to a curious sight. Some distance from shore, she observed several bathers standing in water that came up to their ankles; but closer to shore, several bathers stood in water up to their waists or chests.

A sandbar, Lucy realized.

The discovery delighted her. She waited for the bathers on the sandbar to depart, then ran into the water and when it got deep enough, dove in and swam to the sandbar.

Upon reaching the sandbar she climbed onto it and stood, her arms outstretched. She wiped the salt from her eyes and flipped back her hair. She looked in all directions, turning on the sandbar 360 degrees. She felt she was hovering above everything around her at a great height, even though she knew it was only a few feet. Everywhere she saw ocean, sand, and fleshy people, and it all struck her as beautiful.

She heard the sound of water sloshing and turned to see George Emison, as naked as she, rising from the ocean, climbing up upon the sandbar, and coming towards her with a garland of bluebonnets.

"Lucy," he said, "I was hoping I'd find you. I saved these for you. May I?"

Lucy nodded, and gasped and held her breath as George put the garland over her head.

"Thank you," Lucy whispered, her voice caught in her throat.

"You look very beautiful," George said.

Lucy had been marching down the beach only minutes earlier, hoping to find George and befriend him . Now that she had found him, she no longer knew what to do with him.

George looked at her, smiling. After a moment, the smile disappeared, although he continued to look at her, only now, quite seriously.

Lucy didn't know what this meant, but she thought it probably mattered.

She let her eyes momentarily wander over George, from head to ankle.

God, he was handsome, she thought.

And then she kissed him.

She wasn't quite sure how it happened. She wasn't even sure she made the first move. She thought she had. She had seen him move towards her, and the next thing she knew she took his face in her hands and they were kissing.

And then their bodies were pressed together and they were still kissing. On a sandbar, hovering above everybody else.

And his hand held her lower back, powerfully.

She felt everything around her swirl away. She supposed this is what the old books described as a swoon.

And then she heard Charlotte calling, "Lucy! Oh, Lucy!"

Slowly, Lucy and George broke from their kissing. They continued to hold one another, and look into one another's eyes. Lucy felt his arms strong where she held him and felt his hands strong against her back where he held her.

"Lucy," Charlotte cried. "There's a severe weather alert!"

Finally, Lucy looked to shore to see Charlotte, the only one clothed on the beach, waving around her cell phone.

Just then a *ka-boom* of thunder exploded above their heads, the wind picked up alarmingly, and a bolt of lightning struck the dunes.

"We'd better find our things," George said, and Lucy, reluctantly, agreed.

Everyone ran back to where they had left their things, hastily gathered them, and ran for shelter.

Lucy, Charlotte, and George found Ms. Lavin, the Miss Alans, and Izzy, and everyone gathered their clothes, towels, beach bags, and assorted items and ran to a picnic shelter with a thatched roof. Everyone but Charlotte clutched their clothing in a bundle, naked now not to sunshine and gentle breezes, but to lashing wind, which carried with it stinging grains of sand.

"Well, intrepid explorers," Ms. Lavin said. "We can go no farther without clothing our nakedness. We will get soaked, but we have to make a break for the hotel, because this shelter will soon fly away with the storm."

Clumsily, everyone struggled into their clothes, and then ran for the hotel. George and Izzy took up the rear, helping the Miss Alans along.

By the time they got to the lobby, they were every one of them good and soaked, and after much laughter at what everyone deemed a close-call, they agreed to meet later for drinks after hot baths and fresh clothes.

Charlotte insisted that Lucy get the bathroom first, and although Lucy did not want to give Charlotte a reason to play long-suffering martyr, she knew it was hopeless to argue.

Afterwards, once she she was clean and warm, Lucy left the bathroom and walked out onto the balcony to watch the storm.

"Lucy," Charlotte said. "You're still naked."

"Yes," Lucy said. "That's true." She had decided she wasn't going to spend any more time catering to Charlotte's sensitivities.

"Are you going to become one of those roommates who walks around naked all the time?' Charlotte said, jokingly.

"Yes," Lucy confessed, seriously. "I think I am."

Charlotte did not seem pleased to hear it. "Well, I can see your shoulders and your tush got a little too much sun, so maybe it's for the best, for now, to let your skin cool off in the air," Charlotte

47

said. "But for Pete's sake, come in off the balcony."

"I want to watch the storm," Lucy said.

"But people will see you standing at the balcony like that."

"There's no one outside to see me," Lucy said. "They're all hiding from the storm. And who cares if they did?"

"Well, don't get electrocuted," Charlotte said, and went into the bathroom.

Lucy watched the storm, streaks of lightning cracking above the ocean. The balcony was sheltered, so she only got a little bit of spray from the rain when the wind shifted directions.

She was still standing there when Charlotte returned, wrapped in a fluffy, hotel bathrobe.

"How's the storm?" Charlotte asked.

"Magnificent," Lucy said.

Charlotte stood beside her.

"Are we going to talk about it?" Charlotte said. "And don't say 'talk about what?'"

"I don't see how it's something you need to concern yourself with," Lucy said.

"Lucy, you were kissed and embraced while naked by a stranger who was also naked!"

"His name is George," Lucy said. "He's not a stranger. And I kissed him, first."

"What about Cecil?" Charlotte asked, sensibly.

Lucy was thoughtful.

"I'm not sure yet," she admitted.

As she got dressed, Lucy noticed her cell phone was overflowing with texts and notifications. Most of them had something or other to do with the virus. She put the phone in her pocket without reading the texts and notifications. She didn't want to deal with reality just now. There would be plenty of time for reality later.

When they finally made it to the bar, they found the Miss Alans sitting at a table with Izzy and Ms. Lavin, attended by Rabbi Bobe and the Reverend Eager. They all appeared to be well-lubricated. The Rabbi seemed to find the stories the Alans, Izzy, and Ms. Lavin were recounting to be of the utmost hilarity. The Reverend, judging by his stern expression, seemed to feel the opposite.

George was sitting by himself at the bar.

"You sit with the group," Lucy instructed Charlotte. "I'm going to talk to George."

"What are you going to say to him?" Charlotte asked.

"I haven't figured that out yet," Lucy admitted.

"Do you want my help?" Charlotte said.

"Abso-freaking-lutely not," Lucy said, firmly.

Lucy took the seat at the bar next to George and ordered a Jameson on the rocks.

"Thank you for the bluebonnet garland today," Lucy said.

"You're very welcome," George said. He smiled. He seemed pleased to see her.

"I keep thanking you," Lucy said. "It would seem I have a lot for which to be thankful to you."

"You don't have to thank me," George said, modestly. "I'm glad I could be of some assistance."

"Yes, well. Thank you all the same."

"You're welcome."

Lucy shifted in her chair and cleared her throat. "I had a very good time on the beach today."

"I did too," George said, smiling.

Did he mean that in a sexual way, a romantic way, or a recreational way, Lucy wondered? Was it the kiss he enjoyed, or the day at the beach?

"I ran into your father, earlier," she said. "On the beach. He asked me to be your friend."

"I'd like that very much," George said.

"I think I would, too," Lucy said. "Only . . . I want to be sure we don't get ahead of ourselves."

George raised an eyebrow. "Yes?" he said inviting her to go on.

She shouldn't have to go on, she thought. Why did men always not get it?

"I mean," Lucy stammered," I mean, on the sandbar . . ."

"Yes?"

"When we . . ."

"When we kissed?" George offered, helpfully.

Lucy cleared her throat. "Yes. That."

"Yes?" George said.

Damn him, Lucy thought. He just keeps pressing and pressing.

"Well, you know," Lucy said. "The sunshine. The ocean. Our . . ."

"Our nakedness?"

Lucy hurried past that clarification. "I just think I got kind of carried away."

"We both did."

"But I don't want you to think . . . to presume . . ."

"I wouldn't make any presumptions."

"Because there are . . . complications."

"Ok,"

"There's . . . someone else."

"Ok," George said.

"So, I don't want you to think . . ."

"I understand," George said. "We won't bring it up again." He smiled. "Unless you decide you want me to."

So, it was all on her, now? Lucy thought.

Lucy's cell phone buzzed.

She looked at the number. It was her mother.

"Excuse me," Lucy said, climbing down off the bar stool. "I have to take this."

Lucy spoke to her mother as she walked out of the bar and into the lobby.

"Lucy," her mother said. "I need you to come home immediately and pick up your brother from college on your way."

It was such an odd way to begin a conversation, that Lucy hesitated for a moment before offering a reply, to make sure she fully processed what was being asked of her.

"Lucy, sweetie?" her mother said, in response to her daughter's uncharacteristic silence. "Are you there? Hello? Can you hear me? Did I lose you?"

"Is Freddy in trouble?" Lucy asked. "Did he get expelled?"

"No, of course not," her mother said. "Well, I mean, I guess that's not beyond the realm of possibility, it is your brother we're talking about after all. But no, in this case, Freddy didn't do anything silly to get himself expelled. I mean, I'm sure he did things that are silly, but he's not being expelled."

"So, why do I have to pick him up?"

"Because they're closing down the campus, sweetie," Ms. Haimowitz said.

50

"Closing it down?"

"Yes, dear. The whole campus. Classes are moving on-line."

"Because of the plague ships?" Lucy asked.

"The plague ships?" her mother said, confused.

"The cruise ships with the virus docking on the West Coast," Lucy clarified.

"Yes, well, it is the same virus on those ships, but it's on both coasts now, as well as points in between," her mother said.

"Does Freddy have it?"

"Freddy is fine," Ms. Haimowitz said. "As far as anyone knows, no one on campus has it. But colleges are closing down and moving to on-line courses all over the country. They say it's only going to be for a few weeks, but people are saying they won't likely re-open for the rest of the semester. You need to get Freddy and meet us at the weekend house. We'll wait it out there. It's much safer than the city. Cecil's here. We invited him to quarantine with us, since his family is so far away."

"Cecil's there?"

"Yes, we're all going to hunker down together. The governor is closing down the state, so we need to get moving. Other states are sure to follow."

"How do you close down a state?"

"It's called a Stay at Home Order. He's closed the schools, the theatres, restaurants, concert halls. Didn't you watch the news today?"

"I was on the beach."

"Well, I'm glad you had fun. Now hurry home."

"What about my return flight?"

"Forget the flight. You'll need to rent a car and drive to pick up your brother. No worries, I'll reimburse you."

"Ok," Lucy said, in a daze.

"Don't forget Charlotte," her mother said. "She can stay with us at Lake Eden, too."

PART TWO:
They Return, Diverted Along the Golden and Emerald Motorways

This was how Lucy and Charlotte wound up driving with the Emisons to pick up Freddy.

By the time Lucy returned to the bar, everybody was in an uproar. Tweets, notifications, and texts had suddenly alerted them all to the necessity of cutting vacations short and re-arranging travel plans. The Rabbi, Reverend Eager, the Miss Alans, and Ms. Lavin were all able to change their flights, in some cases with steep fines, to flights the next morning. Lucy and Charlotte, however, were not able to find an available rental car anywhere.

"We have a car!" Izzy shouted. "Tell them George, tell them we have a car!"

"We have a car," George agreed.

"It's a van," Izzy clarified. "Three rows of seats, plenty for all of us and your brother in addition! We're all going to the same place! I'm going to be up at Lake Eden working on my memoirs!"

"Are you really?" Lucy said. "That sounds intriguing. George, what will you be doing?"

"Helping my dad," George said. "And swimming in Lake Eden. You should ride with us."

"We couldn't impose on you like that," Charlotte said, leaving Lucy to wonder how she thought they were going to pick up Freddy without a car. Wait a week, or maybe divert their scheduled airline flight?

"It's no imposition at all," Izzy declared. "George, tell them it's no imposition!"

"It's no imposition," George affirmed.

"But Freddy's college would be out of your way," Charlotte protested.

"We really don't mind," George said.

"George! Tell them they should go with us!" Izzy demanded.

"It's so obvious they should," George said, "there really isn't anything else to say."

And so, early the next day, they threw their things into the back of the van and, with George at the wheel, began the journey to Lake Eden, with a stop planned to pick up Freddy.

"Is your bottom still sunburned, Lucy?" Izzy asked.

"Dad," George gently admonished.

"Excuse me?" Lucy said.

"It's a long ride to be sitting on a sunburned bottom," Izzy said. "And yours was starting to look a little pinkish yesterday."

Lucy would normally have been quite put out to have an old man making comments like this, but there was something so guileless and naïve about Mr. Emison, that she decided to let it pass.

"I'm quite all right, thank you, Mr. Emison – "

"Izzy!"

"Izzy," Lucy corrected herself. "But if it bothers me, I'll have Charlotte apply an ointment."

Charlotte's eyes widened and the look she gave Lucy announced she was not looking forward to applying any ointment anywhere.

"We have just the ointment!" Izzy announced. "It has aloe in it!"

"If we need it," Lucy assured him, "we won't hesitate to ask."

"Ok, Dad," George said. "We can stop talking about bottoms and ointments now."

"Everyone has a bottom," Izzy mused, philosophically. "Why should that make us ashamed?"

Philosophically, Lucy agreed, but felt the topic of her own bottom had exceeded the limits of casual conversation. Her sunburn, which she had not even remembered she had until Izzy brought it up, was starting to make sitting uncomfortable, and they were only a few miles into their journey.

The traffic was surprisingly normal. Lucy wondered how much had occurred in the rest of the world while she had been on the beach. She had yet to scroll through the backlog of notifications glaring at her from her phone's screen.

Although the traffic was normal, every highway rest stop was closed, presumably as a precaution to prevent crowds and the transmission of the virus. It didn't appear to have been a very well thought out policy, however. On the shoulder of the highway, stretching for miles back from the rest stop entrances, long-haul truckers in their eighteen wheelers were lined up, having nowhere else to go to take a break.

This meant Lucy, Charlotte, and the Emisons couldn't eat or get gas themselves without pulling off the highway, which they did after dark.

All the service stations near the highway were closed. They drove twelve miles into a small town before they found a working gas pump, an almost empty diner, and a small motel, its décor seemingly made up almost entirely of plastic furnishings, where they spent the night.

It rained all that night, booms of thunder shaking their bedframes, flashes of lightning illuminating their darkened rooms, pelting raindrops pounding the windows.

The next morning, as they availed themselves of free muffins and coffee, the desk clerk said, "you won't be getting back onto the highway today, I'm afraid. Road's flooded out."

They consulted their mobile phones for alternate routes and came up with nothing.

"Do we have to wait out the flooding?" Lucy asked.

"Could be some time," the desk clerk said. "Last time it took a week before the roads re-opened."

The desk clerk helpfully produced an old-fashioned, paper road map, and laid it out on the desk for them. Lucy explained to him where they were going.

"Now, if you follow this road here," he said, tracing his finger along a tiny line running away from the highway, "that'll take you to the Golden Interstate Motorway, which heads in the same direction as the highway." He traced is finger along another small line that headed roughly in the same direction as the highway, but along a winding, leisurely route. "Takes you right through dairy country. That's why they call it the Golden Motorway. Because of the butter. They were gonna call it the Buttery Interstate Motorway, but cooler heads prevailed. It'll take you right to your brother's college. It's a damn sight more scenic route than the highway, too."

"If you like cows," Charlotte grumbled.

"Can we get back on the highway, eventually?" Lucy asked.

"Well, now, that's an interesting question," the man said. "You got a lot of wetlands between the Golden Motorway and the highway, so the roads in between could well all be flooded out. I'd say your best bet would be to take the Golden Interstate Motorway direct to your destination. It'll take a little longer, but it'll get you there."

"How much longer?" Lucy asked.

"Well, that depends," the man said.

"Depends on what?" Charlotte asked impatiently.

"How fast you drive," the desk clerk said, ticking the possibilities on his finger. "If you don't get stuck behind a stray cow; and if you don't get pulled over."

As they drove, the skies cleared, and arcing over the landscape they saw a vivid, brilliant rainbow.

"It's a double rainbow," Charlotte noted. And it was.

Spontaneously, George and Lucy sang Jimmy's Fallon's comedic song "Double Rainbow," a Neil Young parody. Even more surprisingly, they both knew all the words, which were essentially transcribed from a viral youtube video of a man named Paul "Bear" Vasquez, who a few years previously had been recorded enthusiastically commenting upon his own sighting of a double rainbow.

All around them for hours they saw dairy cows grazing in open fields. Places to stop and gas up were few and far between. In a town called "Witch's Kneecap" they found a service station and bought sandwiches at a nearby roadside sandwich shack called "The Witch's Kneecap Roadside Sandwich Shack," where they ordered their food at a window and ate it at picnic tables set out front.

They lost about an hour when, in fact, they got stuck behind some errant cows who had wandered onto the road through a hole in a fence.

After dark it began to rain again, pelting the windshield with such ferocity that Lucy, at the wheel, was momentarily blinded between each desperate sweep of the wiper.

Up ahead, through the rain, they could just make out a giant crucifix. As they got closer, they could see there was a figure of Jesus attached to it.

"Well, will you look at that?" Izzy said. "Jesus is watching over us."

"We must be in Bible country," George said.

"I just hope we're not in KKK country," Charlotte said.

As they got closer, Lucy said, "Jesus is wearing a surgical mask."

Sure enough the figure on the cross was wearing a surgical mask.

Then the figure moved.

"Did you see that?" Lucy whispered.

Charlotte was the only one who had seen it.

"I'm pulling over," Lucy announced.

Over Charlotte's protestations, Lucy pulled the car over. She put it in park and got out, standing in the pelting rain, looking up at the figure on the cross.

"Hello?" she called.

George was standing beside her.

"Hello!" called back Jesus from the cross.

"Are you all right?" Lucy asked.

"Why, I'm just fine, Ma'am, but thank you for asking," Jesus said. "I ain't nailed to this thing or nothing. I'm just sorta perched here."

"But . . . why?" Lucy asked. She was beginning to think this person on the cross wasn't actually Jesus.

"Well, as a sign of our community's reverence for Christ Our Savior and in an effort to double-up His protective cloak of love to ward off the plague that is plaguing our God-fearing nation under God," said the man who wasn't Jesus.

By now Lucy was soaked through and her wet hair was hanging in her eyes.

"Could I persuade you to come down, though?" Lucy said. "I

don't think it's very healthy or safe for you to be up there in the rain."

"Oh, I'm just fine, thank you," the man said.

A bolt of lightning cracked through the sky, briefly illuminating everything. Lucy could see the man was young, skinny, and wore only a loincloth and a facemask. He lacked his Savior's beard and long hair, however.

"Could I convince you to reconsider?" Lucy said. "I don't think the savior would want you to be hit by lightning. Let us give you a ride somewhere."

Another bolt streaked through the sky, its jagged pattern leaving a lingering glow on Lucy's retina. Thunder boomed and Lucy felt it shake her insides.

"Well, maybe I will," the man said. "Just so you don't worry none."

Inside the car, the man kept his mask on, even though he insisted he did not have the virus nor any symptoms. He began to shiver, and Izzy draped a jacket over his shoulders.

Everyone introduced themselves.

"My name is Ray Folger," the man said. "Like the coffee."

"Can we drop you off anywhere?" Lucy asked.

"If you just keep going in the direction you're already heading, you can just drop me off on the side of the road in a couple of miles," Ray said. "Then it's just a couple more miles up a dirt road to my trailer."

Lucy wiped her wet hair from her face, put the car into gear, pulled out onto the road, and felt a chill as her wet clothes stuck to her skin and to the seat beneath her.

"We can take you all the way home, Ray," Lucy said.

"Lulu," Charlotte whispered sharply. "Didn't you ever see *Deliverance?*"

Ray Folger did not give any indication *he* had seen *Deliverance.*

"Jesus will protect us from the virus," Ray said. "I believe that."

"Well, I hope someone does," Lucy said.

"I don't have much in the way of brains," Ray admitted. "But I know what I know."

"Let me tell you what *I* know," Izzy said. "It's a story: The water was rising. An evacuation was ordered. A very pious man waited in his house. A neighbor came by in a jeep and offered him a ride out of the evacuation zone. The man said, 'I am a pious man, the Lord will protect me.' The neighbor drove off, and the water continued to rise. Eventually, the street was flooded. Another neighbor came by in a boat, and offered to give the pious man a ride out of the flood-zone. The pious man said, 'the Lord will protect me.' But the water continued to rise. Eventually, the man had to go upon his roof, the water was up to the second floor of his house. A National Guard helicopter flew over, and dropped down a rope ladder. The man waved it off. 'I am a pious man, the Lord will protect me.' The helicopter flew off. The water continued to rise. Guess what happened next?"

"The Lord protected him?" Ray suggested.

"He drowned," Izzy said.

"Oh no," Charlotte said. Apparently, she was hoping for a different outcome.

"And when the man gets to heaven," Izzy began.

"So, he made it to heaven?" Ray asked.

"He did," Izzy confirmed. "In heaven, he asks God, 'God —'"

"Was it the heavenly Father, or Jesus?" Ray asked. "Or Saint Peter?"

"I'm not sure," Izzy admitted. "I wasn't there. I only heard about it afterwards."

"How did you hear about it afterwards?" Ray asked.

"I'm a journalist," Izzy said. "I have my sources."

That seemed to satisfy Ray Folger.

"So, the pious man says to God, 'I am a pious man, why didn't you save me?' And what do you think God says to him?"

"He says," Lucy, who had heard this story before, offered, "'what are you talking about, I didn't save you? I sent you a jeep, I sent you a boat, I sent you a helicopter! Didn't save you? You rejected my efforts to save you every time!'"

"I knew this girl was smart and wise!" Izzy exclaimed.

"So, what's the moral of the story?" Charlotte asked.

"The Lord helps those who help themselves?" Ray suggested.

"Don't turn away help from your neighbors?" George said.

"God reveals himself through his creations," Lucy said, "when we listen to our better angels."

"All of the above!" Izzy announced.

Lucy saw blue flashing lights in her rear-view mirror.

"Uh-oh," she said, as she pulled over.

"Don't worry none," Ray said. "That's just Sheriff Luddy Ebsen. He's nice enough, but he's got a bad ticker. He's had a couple of heart attacks, and he's got a pace-maker in his chest. His doctors say he needs a new heart. He's also got arthritis. People say his heart went bad after he became a widower. Losing his wife broke his heart."

"That's so sad," Lucy said.

The Sherriff came up the window. Lucy rolled it down, filled with sympathy for the broken-hearted lawman with the pacemaker.

"Evening Ma'am," he said. He was beefy, red-faced, and short of breath. He wore a wide-brimmed sheriff hat with a tin star pinned to the front. Rain pooled on the brim and ran down the front, partly obscuring his face. He turned to Ray Folger. "Hello, Ray."

"Hello, Sherriff," Ray said.

"Ray, were you up on that cross again?"

"I was."

"How many times do I have to tell you that violates about a dozen local ordinances? We'll be lucky if half the cows don't start making sour milk now, out of the shock of fright you gave them, seeing you up there."

"Do cows make sour milk when they get scared?" Charlotte asked.

The Sherriff ignored her. "I thank you good people for convincing Ray to come down from that cross in the middle of a lightning storm. Ray, standing in this rain is making my joints stiff, and the lightning's going to short out my pacemaker if we don't get inside my Crown-Vic and let me give you a ride home now."

"Sure," Ray said. "That'd be swell."

Ray climbed out of the van and into the police car.

After they drove off, Charlotte said, "do you think he had the virus?"

"Let's hope not," Lucy said. "Because if he did, then we probably all do."

After two more hours on the road, the rain had stopped, Lucy's clothes were still damp and she was still chilled, and everyone had to pee, badly.

The first gas station they pulled into was closed.

"Let's see if the restrooms are open," Charlotte suggested.

The restrooms were not open.

"Let's use the woods," Lucy said. She pointed. "Boys, that way, girls, this way."

They trudged off in their appropriately gendered directions.

"I can't pee in the woods," Charlotte complained.

"If you have to pee badly enough, you can pee in the woods," Lucy pointed out.

"What if there's a bear?" Charlotte said.

"Always check the spot you're going to pee on, and make sure there's not a bear on it," Lucy said.

"I don't mean directly under me, I mean around the area."

"I'll keep a look out for bears while you pee," Lucy said.

"I can't pee with you right there," Charlotte said.

"I'll go somewhere else."

"No!" Charlotte cried. "Don't abandon me! I'll die of fear."

"I'll stand beside you, but I'll look in the other direction."

"Which other direction?"

"The direction from which the bears are coming," Lucy said.

When they decided they had gone deep enough into the woods, they found a steep embankment that dropped down into the dark. They heard what appeared to be a stream running below.

Lucy pulled down her jeans and squatted over the edge.

"You're going to pee down the hill?" Charlotte said, aghast. "What if there's a bear down there?"

"Then you'll have to find somewhere else to pee," Lucy said.

Lucy finished, and told Charlotte it was her turn. "See?" Lucy said. "No bears."

"No bears *yet*," Charlotte said.

Lucy turned her back to allow Charlotte her privacy, and kept a look out for bears.

She heard the rustle of her cousin's pants and the clatter of her belt buckle and then she heard the stream of urine, at first hesitant, then fulsome, and then she heard something give way, heard Charlotte cry out, and then heard the sound of something Charlotte-sized tumbling down a steep embankment and crashing into the stream below.

Lucy slowly turned around.

Charlotte was gone.

"Charlotte?" she called, uncertainly.

"Help me!" Charlotte cried from below.

Lucy slid down the embankment after her cousin, grabbing onto trees and limbs for support, sliding down the steep, muddy slope with her sneakers first and her hip in the soil.

When she reached the stream, she found Charlotte, her pants around her ankles, standing in the stream, covered in mud from head to toe.

"Oh," Lucy said. "Poor Charlotte."

"I went in face first!" Charlotte cried.

The stream was as much a fast-moving mudslide as it was a stream, Lucy noticed.

"I can see that you did," Lucy said.

"I rolled head over heels down the hill and peed all over myself!"

"Oh, no," Lucy said, sympathetically, but then struggled to contain a guffaw.

"Are you laughing at me?" Charlotte demanded.

"Not at all," Lucy said, and laughed.

"It's not funny!"

"It's not," Lucy agreed, laughing.

"You are the worst!" Charlotte said.

"I am," Lucy admitted, as her laughter subsided, if only just. "I am the absolute worst."

Charlotte waited until her cousin had fully stopped laughing, which took several additional moments, after which Lucy still struggled to stifle her mirth.

"What am I going to do?" Charlotte said.

"Pull up your pants," Lucy said.

But Charlotte's pants were around her ankles and beneath the mud slide.

"My clothes are filthy with mud and muddy water and I've peed all over myself!" Charlotte cried.

"Oh, dear," Lucy said. "You've peed all over yourself, have you?"

Lucy began to laugh again.

"I'm glad you think this is so funny," Charlotte said.

"You stay here," Lucy suggested. "I'll bring you a fresh change of clothes."

"I'm not staying here!" Charlotte said. "What about the bears?"

"We haven't actually established there are any bears," Lucy pointed out.

"I don't want to be standing down here all by myself when we do," Charlotte said.

"Ok," Lucy said. "We can climb up the hill, go back to the car, get a fresh change of clothes, and we can change behind the abandoned gas station. I need to get out of these wet things, anyway."

Charlotte didn't seem to like the idea, but she didn't suggest another. She reached down and began to pull up her pants.

"My clothes are caked with mud," Charlotte complained. "Inside and out!"

"You're going to have to squish around in muddy underpants for a bit, I think," Lucy said.

"I can't do that!" Charlotte insisted. "What if there's leeches in all this muck?"

Good point, Lucy thought.

"Well," Lucy said, struggling mightily to contain her laughter, newly rising. "There's only one other way I can think to make this work."

It was this final option that resulted in Lucy, Charlotte's muddy clothes bundled under an arm, trudging up the hill, grabbing ahold of the tree limbs with her free hand, pulling herself ever upwards, alongside Charlotte, now completely naked but for her sneakers and the thick mud that caked her body, doing likewise, but with the benefit of two good hands.

When at last they reached the crest, they were greeted by George, who said, "oh, there you are. I was getting worried."

Charlotte's immediate reaction was to shriek and start, which caused her to lose her balance. Lucy reached out to her, but too late. Charlotte tumbled backward and rolled head over heel down the muddy embankment yet again, shrieking all the way, disappearing into the dark, ending in a loud splash.

George appeared quite alarmed and immediately began to slide down the hill after her.

Lucy, unable to contain her laughter, followed.

At the bottom of the ravine, she found Charlotte, again standing ankle deep in the stream, her body covered with yet more mud which now also covered her face and saturated her hair, hanging from strands in thick, wet clumps. She was howling with sobs. George stood ankle deep in the water with her, an arm around her shoulders, trying to comfort her.

Lucy burst into even more laughter, quite uncontrollably.

George looked at her in horror.

Charlotte stopped her sobbing long enough to also look at her cousin in horror.

Still, Lucy could not stop snorting with laughter.

And then, through the muddy coating that covered her face, Lucy saw Charlotte's white teeth as her cousin opened her mouth and joined her in the laughter.

George at first looked quite confused, looking back and forth between the two now-mirthful cousins, before their merriment overcame him, and he began to laugh as well.

When at last they found their way back to the gas station, George resourcefully found a hose with the water still running. Behind the gas station, out of view of Izzy who, despite his philosophies, seemed to understand his presence would mortify poor Charlotte even more than she had been mortified already, the three of them took off what muddy clothes they still wore and sprayed each other's bare bodies down with freezing cold water until they were all clean, steam rising from their flesh, their skin ruddy from the water's spray and the evening's chill.

Charlotte kept her eyes closed tight the entire time.

It occurred to Lucy that the only thing that traumatized Charlotte more than other people viewing her nakedness was her viewing the nakedness of others.

Lucy found this rather sad.

They dressed in dry clothes and resumed their journey.

They found a working gas pump ten miles on, filled up the tank and stocked up on stale gas station sandwiches and snacks, resumed their course, and drove through the night, taking turns at the wheel. Charlotte, thoroughly traumatized by her tumbles, mud-soaking, and unanticipated nakedness, fell asleep by herself in the third row of seats and did not wake until dawn.

At noon, they picked up Freddy from college. They found him waiting in front of his dorm on a nearly deserted campus, a few students still walking the grounds, about half of them wearing surgical face masks. Freddy did not wear a mask but, upon introductions, offered to rub elbows rather than shake hands, a new custom to which Lucy had not yet been alerted.

They loaded up the back of the van with Freddy's things – his duffle, laptop, guitar, ukulele, and backpack. They gassed up at an open service station, again loaded up on stale sandwiches, and continued the drive. They tried to get back on the interstate highway, but discovered it was still closed to traffic – rather than flooding, this time the cause was some kind of chemical spill. They made their way back to the Golden Interstate Motorway, and continued onward in the direction of Lake Eden. They again took turns driving, but after Freddy's shift, it was universally agreed he would not again be allowed behind the wheel.

They drove on until the orange warning light came on announcing they were low on fuel. After a nervously long time, as the needle crept ever lower, they finally came upon a working gas station.

A young, muscularly wiry man came bounding up to the car and announced his name was Leon and it would be his pleasure to fulfill their service station needs. He actually wore an old-fashioned service station uniform and cap. He appeared to be out of the previous century.

Lucy watched in awe as Leon filled the gas tank, checked the tires, checked the oil, and in general made her feel as if the van they were driving in was the most important vehicle in the world. Lucy could not remember the last time she had stopped at a full-service station, much less one so thorough.

"Anything else I can do for you, Ma'am?" Leon said. "We have sandwiches and soda pop."

"Do you have bathrooms?" Lucy asked. It had been a while since the fiasco of the embankment.

"I'm afraid not," Leon said. "Bathrooms are out of order. We don't even have employee bathrooms. There's a porta-potty out back, but I wouldn't use it if I were you for anything less than a global emergency, if you know what I mean. They don't clean it out all that often. You're free to pee on the grass out back of the station, if you want. I'll show you a good spot and then leave you to your privacy."

Lucy looked to Charlotte. Charlotte shook her head decisively, indicating a hard "no." After the trauma of the last alternative restroom, this was not something she wanted to contemplate.

"We'll wait," Lucy told Leon.

"Could be a ways down the road before you find something," Leon said.

"We'll take our chances," Lucy said.

"Suit yourselves," Leon said. "Say, do you mind if I ask you something?"

"Not at all," Lucy said.

"Are you folks from the city?"

"We are," Lucy admitted. "How did you know?"

"He can tell we're Jews," Freddy said. "Rural goyim have a sixth sense about these things."

"Um, no, it was actually your license plate," he said, uncomfortably. "Used to be, my grand-folks tell me, this was the only way through these parts until Eisenhower built the interstate system. Used to be city folk coming through here all the time. Aside from Route Sixty-Six, the Golden Interstate Motorway was the best way to travel across the country, they said. It's a lot quieter now."

"Well," Lucy said, "the Golden Interstate Motorway certainly does have its charms."

"I'd like to show you something," Leon said, digging into his back pocket, "if you don't mind."

He handed Lucy a crumpled letter. Lucy took the letter, smoothed it out, and began to read.

"Why, Leon," she said. "You've been accepted to college."

"Congratulations, boyo!" Izzy cried from the backseat.

"Well done," George added.

"That's lovely," Charlotte said, unconvincingly.

"Don't do it," Freddy moaned. "Save yourself, before it's too late."

"The thing of it is," Leon said, uncertainly, "I don't know if I should go."

Charlotte perused the letter. "Leon," she said. "You're getting a free ride. Of course you should go."

"The truth is, the farthermost I've ever been from home is the county fair," he admitted.

"Did they have butter sculptures?" Freddy asked.

"Of course," Leon said.

"I tried to make a butter sculpture of my girlfriend once, but I ran out of butter," Freddy said. "She was quite *zaftig*, and I mean that in the best possible way. So, we used it for . . . well, if you watch *Last Tango in Paris*, you'll know what we used it for."

"Freddy, that's enough," Charlotte snapped.

"I've never seen *Last Tango in Paris*," Leon said.

"Ignore my brother," Lucy told Leon. "He's a deviant. You were saying?"

"Well, I've only ever seen the college campus on-line," Leon said. "I've never even visited."

"Are you worried about being homesick?" Lucy asked.

"Not homesick so much," Leon said. "The campus is three hours away, so I could come back for Thanksgiving and such easy enough."

"Come home as rarely as possible," Freddy advised. "That way you won't have to sober up as often."

"Got a girl, Leon?" Izzy asked, sympathetically.

Leon nodded. "She went off to college."

Lucy held up the letter. "Same college?"

Leon nodded.

"She waiting for you to join her?" Lucy asked.

"She emails me all the time," Leon said. "She tells me everything about it."

"Do you love her?" Lucy asked.

"I do," Leon admitted.

"Does she love you?" Charlotte asked. She seemed to be getting into the spirit of things.

"She tells me she does every day," Leon said.

"Do you believe her?" Lucy said.

"She's never given me any reason not to," Leon said.

"Then what are you waiting for?" George said, impatiently. "You have a free ride and a girl you love and who loves you in turn waiting for you, and a world of limitless possibilities in front of you."

"Maybe he prefers the company of cows?" Freddy suggested. "Or maybe he's working on a life-size butter sculpture of a cow."

"I'm concerned I won't fit in," Leon said.

"With the cows?" Freddy asked.

"On campus," Leon clarified.

"I think the butter sculptures will be quite the chick-magnet on campus, actually," Freddy said.

"What's your girl's name, Leon?" Lucy asked.

"Bertie," Leon said. "Bertie Lahr."

"Does Bertie fit in to college life?" Lucy said.

"Bertie's more worldly than I am," Leon said. "She's got a digital subscription to the *New Yorker*."

"Don't worry about fitting in," Izzy said. "Be your own man! Let those collegiate co-eds fit in with you and Bertie!"

"It's just, to be honest," Leon said. "I always planned on eventually inheriting the service station from Dad, and I'm not sure I need a college education to do that."

"That's a fine ambition," Freddy said, "and an excellent point."

"But Leon," Lucy said. "You mustn't think of the utility of a college-education in merely practical terms," Lucy said. "You must think about it in *enriching* terms. College will enrich your life. Why shouldn't the master of this service station read *Anna Karenina*?"

"I've read *Anna Karenina*," Leon said. "The Garnett translation and the Pevear/Volokhonsky, both."

"Which do you like better?" George asked.

"Well, the Garnett is essential reading to understand its influence on mid-20th century authors like Hemingway and Mailer," Leon said. "But the Pevear/Volokhonsky is the better read."

"Oh God," Freddy groaned. "He's a college boy already."

"Leon," Lucy said, "you will fit in perfectly."

Leon smiled. "You know what? I think you're right. I'm going to email them my acceptance as soon as my shift ends."

"Yes!" Izzy shouted loudly, causing Charlotte to cover her ears. "What do I always say, George?"

"Never trust an enterprise that requires the wearing of clothes?" George said.

"No, not that, the other thing!"

"By the side of the everlasting *Why,*" George said, wearily, "there is a *Yes.*"

"Good for you son!" Izzy shouted to Leon. "Good for you for embracing the *Yes*! You and Bertie will be very happy!"

It was a good two hours additional drive before they found a place to stay for the night, and to pee: an old-fashioned motor lodge with charming, if somewhat under-maintained, individual cabins.

Later, as Izzy, Freddy, George, and Lucy drank rum from plastic, disposable cups, sitting on wooden chairs in a grassy clearing in front of the cabins, they heard Charlotte scream in horror. They all ran inside, prepared to rescue her from whatever apparent dreadfulness had befallen her.

They found her standing naked in front of a three-way mirror, her back to the mirror, her neck craning for a better look. When she saw everybody staring at her in confusion and concern, she screamed again and ran into the bathroom, locking the door behind her.

Lucy rapped impatiently at the bathroom door.

"Lotte!" Lucy called, crossly. "If you don't want everyone to see you without your clothes on, stop screaming all the time when you haven't got your clothes on!"

"I've got a tick on my tushie!" Charlotte called back.

Lucy and Freddy exchanged glances and tried not to laugh. Lucy succeeded in this endeavor, but Freddy did not.

"Ticks can actually be quite serious, you know," Lucy admonished.

Freddy ignored her. "Wait here," he said.

Freddy left the room and returned a few moments later. He handed Lucy a pair of surgical gloves and a surgical mask. "Put these on," he said.

"Is Lotte infected with the virus?" Lucy asked.

"It's just a precaution," Freddy said.

"Where did you get these?" Lucy asked.

"I carry them with me everywhere I go," Freddy said. "For tick checks."

Lucy put on the mask and gloves.

"Charlotte," Freddy called into the door. "Open the door. I will remove the tick. I have tweezers."

Freddy took a set of tweezers from his Swiss Army knife.

"Give them to Lulu!" Charlotte cried.

"I can give them to Lulu," Freddy said. "But this is a two-person operation. Would you like me to ask George or Izzy?"

"It's not a two-person operation," Lucy whispered to her brother. "You're just trying to embarrass Charlotte."

"Of course I am," Freddy whispered back. "She makes it so much fun."

After a moment, Charlotte opened the door a crack and peered out. She was wrapped in a towel. Freddy handed her a surgical mask. Charlotte put it on.

"Brace yourself against the sink," Freddy ordered. "Stand with your feet shoulder-length apart. This is a deadly serious business. Remember, I'm treasurer of the Student Camping Association, so I know all about tick bites."

Charlotte did as instructed, bravely standing with her arms braced on the edge of the sink and her feet shoulder-length apart.

Freddy turned to George. "You wait here," he told him. "I may need you."

George waited while Izzy beat a hasty retreat, understanding that Charlotte was uncomfortable enough with only her cousins and George there, much less Izzy Emison.

Freddy and Lucy entered the bathroom and shut the door behind them.

Freddy pulled the towel off Charlotte. Charlotte shrieked.

"No false modesty, Charlotte," Freddy scolded her. "I can't work with this towel in my way."

"Freddy!" Charlotte cried, flailing about as she tried to cover herself with her hands.

"Shush now," Freddy said. "I'm pre-med."

For whatever reason, that reassured Charlotte enough to stop protesting. She braced herself once more against the sink, shut her eyes tightly, and held her breath as Freddy knelt down to examine her buttocks.

"That's a tick, alright," he said. "A deer tick, too. It's big, though, so you probably don't have Lyme. The smaller ones are usually the carriers. Lulu, daub a washcloth in your cup of rum."

Lucy retrieved her Dixie cup of rum. She did as instructed, and handed the washcloth to her brother. Freddy daubed the washcloth on the tick and the surrounding epidermis.

"Pull the skin taught for me, Lucy," Freddy said. He seemed quite serious, and for a moment, Lucy wondered if he actually knew what he was doing.

Lucy put her gloved fingers to either side of the tick and pulled the skin taught.

Freddy meticulously slid the tongs of the tweezers between the tick's pincers and its head, and pulled slowly.

The flesh pulled back with the tweezers before the tick came loose and Charlotte's skin snapped back.

"Well, look at that," Freddy said. "I got the head, too. You can see a little strip of skin still in its jaws."

"Oh, God," Charlotte exclaimed.

"Be still," Freddy said. He emptied he plastic wastebasket onto the floor, dropped the tick into it, and instructed Lucy to continue to hold the skin taught. Then he opened a magnifying glass from his Swiss Army knife and examined the spot where the tick had been.

"You can see the two teeth marks," he said, and handed the magnifying class to Lucy.

Lucy could indeed see two reddish marks where the tick had sunk its pincers.

"Are you done?" Charlotte asked, impatiently.

"No," Freddy said. "We are not."

Freddy took the washcloth and cup of rum, daubed the edge of the cloth again, and gently daubed the bitten area with the cloth.

"Ow," Charlotte said.

"If it hurts, that's a good sign," Freddy said. "It means the tick's pain numbing venom is fading."

"Ticks have pain-numbing venom?" Charlotte said.

"Well, venom is the wrong word," Freddy said. "I'll have to check that spot nightly to be on the lookout for infection or a red ring, which could indicate Lyme or another tick-borne illness."

"Can't Lulu check?" Charlotte asked, meekly.

"Lulu wouldn't know what to look for," Freddy said.

"Remember: Treasurer, Student Camping Association. And pre-med. What would you like me to do with the tick?"

"Get rid of it!" Charlotte cried.

"Do you want me to flush it down the toilet?"

"No! What if it crawls back up?"

"I'll figure something out," Freddy said.

"Can I get dressed now?" Charlotte said.

"Certainly not," Freddy said. "We have to do a full body tick check. George! Come in now!"

"Why is George coming in?" Charlotte said, in a panic.

"I need to check all three of you," Freddy said. "You were all down the muddy embankment according to Lulu."

"Check George elsewhere!" Charlotte said.

"Lotte," Freddy said. "I don't intend to do this all night. Let's do it and get it done. I am, after all, pre-med. I know how these things are done."

Charlotte shut her eyes tightly as George entered the room. Freddy handed George a surgical mask as he explained the situation. George put on the mask, and looked at Lucy for confirmation. Lucy shrugged. She supposed a tick check probably was a good idea. And Freddy had been a Boy Scout, so he did know about some of this outdoorsy stuff.

Lucy and Freddy stripped naked, and Charlotte tightly closed her eyes.

It occurred to Lucy once again that the only thing that pained Charlotte more than being seen naked was seeing other people naked. Or maybe it was seeing other people seeing her naked. Lucy wasn't sure. Either way, she thought it was a little sad.

Freddy made a big show over all three of them turning around, lifting arms, pulling hair away from necks, as he examined them all over. He checked behind their ears, on their scalps, behind their knees, around their belt-lines, in each of their belly-buttons, and between each of their thirty collective fingers and each of their thirty collective toes.

Lucy was beginning to wonder if Freddy didn't actually know what he was doing.

He insisted that Lucy and Charlotte lift up their breasts so Freddy could examine underneath them. Charlotte groaned in discomfiture as she did, her eyes closed yet more tightly.

Lucy worried Freddy's joke was veering into cruelty.

Still, the tick check was probably necessary, even if it didn't have to be quite so communal.

Freddy ordered George to lift his penis so Freddy could examine the underside, and then do the same with his testicles. Although George had been quite the gentleman thus far by not looking directly at Charlotte and Lucy as Freddy conducted his examination, Lucy could not help watching this part of the examination attentively.

Using the flashlight function on his phone and his gloved fingers, Freddy checked everyone's pubic hair, and then examined the area where their inner thighs met their groins. It took some convincing before Charlotte permitted this, but Freddy persuaded her it would be preferable to allow the examination than shelter a tick in that sensitive area.

"All right," Freddy said. "Last part of the exam. Grab ankles."

"Our own?' Lucy asked. "Or each other's?"

George stifled a laugh.

They grabbed their own ankles and Freddy carefully inspected the clefts between each of their buttocks, his mobile phone's light illuminating the customarily unilluminated. Charlotte, by this time drained of energy to protest, raised no objection.

"Lulu," Freddy said, as they once again all stood upright. "You've got a sunburn on your butt. I have an ointment. Charlotte can apply it. Or George. Whomever you prefer."

"We can figure that out later," Lucy said.

"Are we done?" Charlotte said, wearily.

"We are," Freddy said. "No more ticks, I am pleased to say."

"Then get out of the bathroom, please!" Charlotte demanded.

Lucy and George grabbed their clothes and Freddy took the wastebasket with the tick inside of it, and they exited the bathroom.

Freddy pulled a plastic laundry bag from the hotel closet and handed it to George. "Put your clothes in here. Do not wear them again until they have been washed with your muddy clothes from the embankment. Ticks can crawl around in there."

George and Lucy did as instructed, while Freddy collected Charlotte's discarded clothing and put it in the laundry bag as well.

Once the suspect clothing was safely contained inside the bag, Lucy and George looked at one another uncertainly.

"Well," Lucy said. "I'm going to get dressed."

"My clothes are in my room," George said.

Freddy handed George a spare towel from the shelf atop the closet. George wrapped it around his waist.

"I'll see you later," he said. "Thank you for the examination, Freddy."

George left the room, taking the laundry bag with him.

As Lucy hastily dressed, she and Freddy broke down in laughter.

Lucy and Freddy could not stop laughing, so once Lucy was fully dressed, they exited the cabin in the hope that Charlotte would not hear them.

"Oh, poor Charlotte," Lucy said, standing outside the cabin. "Why do you torture her like that?"

"Because it's fun," Freddy admitted. "She is so torture-able."

"Was that examination really necessary?" Lucy asked.

"It was," Freddy insisted. "I would not have looked up your butt-hole otherwise, I assure you. You think I enjoyed that?"

"But you didn't need to examine all three of us crowded together in the bathroom like that."

"Of course not," Freddy said. "That was for Lotte's benefit." He looked into the wastebasket. "What should we do with her tick? Keep it as a pet?"

"Absolutely not."

"Stick it in Lotte's bed and see if it bites her on the ass again?"

"Freddy, you're really a terrible, horrible, morally reprehensible person, do you know that?"

"Does that mean you're against it?"

"Can we just kill the damn thing?"

"Charlotte?" Freddy said. "Put her out of her misery?"

"That's not very nice. Charlotte's not miserable."

"She just tries to make the rest of us miserable."

"Give her a chance!" Lucy said. "What's she done wrong since we picked you up?"

"Nothing," Freddy said. "I love Charlotte. But she's too fun not to torment."

"Are you really treasurer of the Student Camping Association?"

"I'm actually treasurer of the Student Outdoor Clothing-Optional Recreation Association," Freddy said. "But camping is one of our activities. So, I didn't lie when I said I need to know about tick bites."

"I believe you know about tick bites," Lucy said. "What I can't believe is that anyone would trust you as treasurer."

"I started out as recording secretary, but they moved me to treasurer because I kept writing the minutes in rhyming couplets."

"And they didn't appreciate that?" Lucy asked.

"Oh, they appreciated that," Freddy said. "But even so, they thought it prudent to move me to a different position."

"Are you really pre-med?"

"This semester I am. We'll see about the next one."

"Can we just kill that tick?"

"Ok," Freddy sighed. "Do you have a cigarette?"

"You know I don't smoke."

"I have a blunt, though," Freddy said.

"Oh," Lucy said. "That's another matter, then."

They fired up the blunt with Izzy and George, and ceremonially put the smoldering end into the fat body of the tick, engorged as it was on Charlotte's blood, until it sizzled and died.

They asked Charlotte to join them for the ritual burning of the tick and the smoking of the blunt, but she declined, opting instead for an early bedtime, owing to the repeated trauma she had suffered ever since they had pulled off the highway the night before.

Early the next morning, Lucy was awakened by a call from her mother.

"Lulu, dear," her mother said. "I need you to turn around and pick up Minnie Bobe."

Sleepily, Lucy asked, "and who is Minnie Bobe?"

"Rabbi Bobe's daughter, of course. She's Freddy age. Her college is also closing up campus and she's got no way to get home. Pick her up and bring her to Lake Eden. Her father is already here and he's very concerned for her. If the Emison's won't drive you, I'll rent you a car."

"The Emison's will probably want to drive us," Lucy said. "They're very generous that way."

The Emison's were more than happy to take the detour and so, after a breakfast of stale coffee, rubbery eggs, and spongy biscuits in the motel dining room, and after waiting for their mud-soaked clothes from the tumble down the embankment and their suspect tick-exposed clothing they had discarded after the tick-check to finish washing and drying, they climbed into the van and started heading back the way they came, veering South after two hours and driving for another three.

When they arrived, Minnie was waiting for them outside her dorm on a campus as nearly deserted as Freddy's. Every other person among those who remained, Lucy noticed, was wearing a face mask.

A bright-eyed, vivacious, petite blond, Minnie was all smiles and bouncy energy as Freddy helped load her things, which included a ukulele, a fancy camera, and an art portfolio, into the back of the van.

"If you need a tick-check, by the way," Freddy told Minnie as they climbed in, "I'm your man."

"He's pre-med," Charlotte said.

"Oh!" Minnie said. "I've always hoped to meet someone who knows how to do a proper tick check."

Lucy didn't know if Minnie was naïve, flirting, or calling his bluff. She could tell by Freddy's face that he didn't know either. She thought maybe that confusion had been Minnie's intention. She thought that she was going to like this girl.

The nearest highway was again closed to traffic, this time because of a ninety-car pile-up that was apparently caused by an overturned hog-hauling eighteen-wheeler. Reports made mentioned of accordioned automobiles and loose hogs for miles in both directions. They checked their road map and made their way to the Emerald Motorway, which lazily twisted its way Northeast, eventually, if the map could be trusted, bringing them closer to Lake Eden.

A few hours after dark, they began to look for a place a stay the night. For miles, the only motels appeared to have been closed for years.

Then, up ahead, on a hill overlooking the motorway, they saw a large building with words in bright green neon: *The Emerald City Casino and Resort.*

"We should stay there," Minnie said.

"They probably have nice rooms," Charlotte said.

"They're probably expensive," Lucy said.

"Your mother will pay," Charlotte reminded her.

Although the lobby and gaming floor were busy and noisy, they did, in fact, have nice rooms available.

After showering and changing, Lucy went down to the pool, but found it closed. A printed sign explained the closure was due to concerns regarding the virus outbreak.

Lucy went back up to her room, changed out of her bathing suit and into something a little more formal, and went down to the casino.

No one seemed to have heard of the virus in the casino. No one was wearing masks. She notice the croupier periodically cleaning down the dice with a disinfectant wipe.

At the roulette table she found Minnie, Freddy, and Charlotte sitting together with a huge pile of chips before them.

Minnie handed Charlotte and Freddy each a small stack of chips. "This is your initial investment back, guys," she said. "Plus a small profit. Pocket that while we're ahead. That way, if we start to lose, we won't be out any of our original cash, so there's no way we can finish at a loss."

Lucy watched with some interest as they continued to win, spin after spin, with Minnie choosing the numbers.

"How do you know?" Charlotte said, amazed. "How do you know what will win?"

"Intuition," Minnie said. "I have good intuition."

They continued to win spin after spin until, finally, they lost two in a row.

"Ok," Minnie said. "We're done."

"No!" Charlotte shouted. "Those were just a momentarily aberration!"

"We should quit while we're ahead," Minnie said.

"I don't want to quit!" Charlotte shouted. "I want to win!"

"Lotte," Minnie said gently. "We're done here. You gotta know when to fold 'em."

Charlotte looked at her with wide, wild eyes.

Finally, her madness seemed to fade and she stood up from the table. Minnie divided their winnings, and they went to cash in.

Freddy lingered a moment.

"Lotte's a big Kenny Rogers fan, I think," he said.

"Did you hear that Kenny Rogers just died?" Lucy said. "I just saw it on the news in my room."

"Of the virus?" Freddy asked.

"No, I don't think so," Lucy said. "It said 'natural causes.'"

"I guess the virus is natural," Freddy said. "Unless it came from a lab."

"Please," Lucy said. "Don't start spreading misinformation."

"Better than spreading the virus."

"Only marginally."

"Poor Kenny," Freddy said. "I guess he really did know when to fold 'em."

"Your girlfriend seems to know her way around a casino pretty well for a Rabbi's daughter," Lucy said.

"She's not my girlfriend." Freddy grinned. "Yet."

"Are you sure you want to date a Rabbinical daughter?" Lucy asked. "Seems like an awful lot of pressure."

"Normally, I'd agree," Freddy said. "But have you looked at her?"

"Did you know Lotte was so susceptible to gambling fever?" Lucy asked.

"That's a Merle Haggard song, I think," Freddy said.

"You're thinking of 'Rambin' Fever,'" Lucy said. "That's what you've got."

"I am restless," Freddy admitted. "Is Merle Haggard still alive?"

"No, sadly."

"Did he die of the virus?" Freddy asked.

"He died in 2016," Lucy said.

"So, that was before the virus," Freddy said. "We think."

"Don't start with the reckless speculation, again," Lucy said. "That's how the seeds of social discord are sown."

"Unless Lotte learns to loosen up and enjoy life a little bit," Freddy said, thoughtfully, "one day she is just going to explode. That edge of hysteria over walking away from the game was just the tip of the iceberg."

Lucy thought, in this case, anyway, Freddy was probably right.

PETER ULLIAN

PART THREE:
The Disaster Without; the Disaster Within; or, A Quarantine with a View

They had been back at Lake Eden for several weeks. Several increasingly strange weeks.

First, unsurprisingly perhaps, Purim was cancelled, as were all religious services for all religions, just like any gatherings anywhere for anything of over ten people.

Then all gatherings were banned of any size whatsoever, and everyone was ordered to stay at home and all non-essential businesses were shuttered. You could go to the grocery store, the drug store, the hardware store, and the liquor store. Maybe a few other stores; Lucy wasn't sure, because all the stores *she* wanted to go to were definitely shuttered. At first, one didn't have to wear a mask when you went to the grocery store. Then everyone had to wear a mask and gloves. Then just a mask, but stay six feet apart. Blue tape on the floor began to appear to tell people where to stand in a line to maintain proper social distancing.

Then there were the new neighbors.

The Emisons, it turned out, had moved in on one side, in a house known as Cissie Villa, while the Rabbi and Minnie had moved in on the other, in a house known as Albert Villa. In between stood the Haimowitz weekend home on Summer Street in the village of Lake Eden, known as Windy Corners.

Since there was so little opportunity to see anyone outside or at home, these three households quickly began to seem like the entire world. They spoke to each other daily over their backyard fences. This seemed to delight Minnie and Freddy, who lit up every time they spoke to one another over the garden fence. The Rabbi didn't appear to be alarmed by this development. Lucy decided he must either be very indulgent of his daughter, or secretly a Reconstructionist.

Lucy, on the other hand, felt increasingly uncomfortable having George in such close proximity every day . . . especially with Cecil there. She had absolutely delightful conversations with George over the garden fence, and every time she did, she felt her heart beat a little faster and her tummy explode into a flittering cascade of butterflies. She found this extremely vexing.

Then, of course, there was Cecil. Cecil was delighted to see Lucy again, but it quickly became obvious he regretted deciding to spend his quarantine in the country with her family. She could feel him feeling the walls closing in.

Her mother, annoyingly, put them up in separate rooms, even though she was 23 and he was 24. Not that Lucy necessarily wanted to spend every night with him. Still, it was annoying that they had to sneak off together to be amorous.

Not that they ever did. Cecil, a germaphobe in normal times, had suggested, reasonably, Lucy thought, that they refrain from carnal embraces until the suggested two-week waiting period had passed, to ensure Lucy hadn't contracted the virus on the long journey home. This coincided with a decision in the household for everyone to avoid kissing and hugging one another, out of an abundance of caution.

The two weeks passed, but the kissing and hugging did not resume, and nor did Cecil and Lucy sneak off together to be amorous. A new normal seemed to have settled on the household. Lucy missed her mother's hugs and kisses, but she did not miss Cecil's. It was not that she no longer had affection for him. But she preferred to refrain from outwardly expressing it while she still struggled to make sense of her feelings for George Emison.

Ironically, even as expressions of physical affection waned, the younger members of three neighboring households began to behave as one extended household, joining together for regular games of badminton in the Haimowitz backyard, which was the largest of the three. Freddy declared this was perfectly acceptable from a medical standpoint, as long as no one broke this three-household "Quarantine Bubble."

Cecil did not participate in these games. Rather, he sat aside in a lawnchair, reading or scrolling the internet on his phone or laptop.

Cecil was also the only one who insisted upon wearing a facemask at all times when he was not alone in his room.

When Passover arrived, it was a Zoom event, and it was surprisingly fun. They connected with family from around the country, and even the Miss Alans joined them, delighted to participate in their young friends' celebration.

After the Seder, as they ate, all in their separate households, the Miss Alans casually mentioned that Reverend Eager had refused to stop holding church services.

Lucy found this alarming.

"Ladies," Lucy said, "you cannot go to church anymore. It is very, very dangerous."

"Yes, I completely agree," Freddy concurred. "And I am pre-med."

"But the Reverend insists it is perfectly safe," said Catherine.

Then Izzy, zooming in from next door, told the story of the pious man in the flood, and his failure to accept the help offered by his fellow man, anticipating some other form of divine intervention that never came.

"That's an excellent parable," the Rabbi said. "May I use it in one of my virtual *d'var Torahs*?"

Lucy and Charlotte continued to do their jobs virtually, and Freddy and Minnie continued their virtual classwork as well. Cecil continued work on his Ph.D. dissertation in the philosophy of something or other. Lucy's mother attended to her gardening with greater vigor than she ever had before. The Rabbi organized a full series of on-line services, giving his congregants a pass on the use of technology on Shabbat, and declaring a proper minyan could be achieved by the gathering of ten or more adult Jews in a virtual space such as a Zoom meeting.

The viral outbreak was officially declared a pandemic. Lucy wasn't entirely clear what made a pandemic a pandemic, but she'd seen enough science fiction movies to know it wasn't a good development. Reports of the rapidly rising death toll around the country, and the overwhelmed hospitals and nursing homes in urban centers, grew increasingly alarming. The United States became the global epicenter of the virus. National leadership proved incompetent and inconsistent, and the effectiveness of state and local response to the pandemic seemed entirely dependent upon whether state and local leadership prioritized lives over capital, or the other way around.

On a day when the weather became suddenly wonderfully warm, Lucy and Cecil went for a hike. Getting outdoors was still allowed, as long as one remained socially distant from anyone not in your household, and wore a mask when one could not.

There was no one on the hiking trail, but Cecil insisted on still wearing his surgical mask. Lucy wore a bandana around her neck in case she needed to pull it up over her nose and mouth, but did not intend to wear it over her face unless they ran into someone.

"You know," Lucy said, as they hiked through the woods, "I can never really think of you in the outdoors."

"I don't really enjoy the outdoors so much, truth be told," Cecil admitted. "There's so many bugs."

"Freddy and I used to spend all summer hiking these woods and swimming in Lake Eden," Lucy said. "We still do, actually."

"At some point, I think," Cecil said, "we all need to put aside childish pursuits."

"Experiencing the natural world is not a childish pursuit, Cecil," Lucy said. "It may be all we have left, if this virus isn't stopped."

"What do you mean by that?"

"Well, the economy has ground to a halt, and we can't do normal things without the risk of dying, and eventually we're all going to get sick and most of us are going to die."

"Most of us are *not* going to die," Cecil said. "Statistically, most of us will survive."

"And those of us who survive, we'll be left with no electricity and no transportation."

"I'm sure that's not going to come to pass."

"We won't be able to make new clothes and we'll run around naked reading old paperback books, playing acoustic instruments, and communing with nature to keep ourselves entertained," Lucy said.

"You have a really idiosyncratic view of the apocalypse," Cecil said.

"I don't think you're going to do very well in the apocalypse, Cecil, and I mean that affectionately," Lucy said.

"You're probably right," Cecil admitted. "Internet is all that's keeping me going as it is."

"Why don't you play badminton in the backyard and go for hikes and swims, like Freddy and I?"

"Freddy and *me*," Cecil gently admonished.

"No, Freddy and *me*," Lucy said. "Not Freddy and *you*. You never do any of those things with Freddy."

"You know what I mean. For a girl who works in publishing, you really should know when to use *I* and when to use *me*," Cecil said.

Lucy considered killing Cecil right then and there. She spied a stone at the side of the hiking path just small enough that she could pick it up, but just big enough that it would probably stove in Cecil's skull quite effectively.

"You make pedantry so damnably charming," Lucy said, instead of killing him.

"I do my best," Cecil said.

"I don't see you in the outdoors, when I imagine you," Lucy said. "I see you in a room. Without a view."

"Without a view?" Cecil protested. "What am I, in prison?"

"No, you're in a regular room, but one without a view."

Cecil though that over.

"When I imagine myself, I'm in a room, and out the window *is* a view," Cecil said.

"And what is the view of?" Lucy asked.

"The view," Cecil said, "is of you."

Lucy was surprised at how flattering she found that. "What do I look like?"

"Like a Leonardo," Cecil said.

"Which one?" Lucy asked.

"*Mary Magdalene*," said Cecil.

"The whore with her boobs out?" Lucy said. "How flattering."

"I guess I'm the room, and you're the view," Cecil said.

Lucy thought that over. "You complete me, Jerry Maguire?" she said.

"Who is Jerry Maguire, again?" Cecil said.

Damn. We were so close, Lucy thought. So close, and yet so far.

They turned a corner on the path, and suddenly Lake Eden, in all its Eden-ish glory, appeared before them.

"This is where Freddy and I swim," Lucy said. "Come into the water with me, Cecil."

"I didn't bring my bathing suit," Cecil said.

"You don't need to bring your bathing suit," Lucy said. "See?"

She pointed to a sign on a tree that read "Clothing Optional Beyond This Point."

Cecil scrutinized the sign.

"Freddy posted this, didn't he?" he said.

"Yes," Lucy admitted. "All around the lake, actually. But that was years ago, and no one's taken them down. So, it must be true."

Lucy began to get undressed.

"Lucy," Cecil protested. "What if someone sees?"

"Then we'll show them the sign," Lucy said.

By the time Lucy was nude, Cecil had only just begun to unlace his shoes.

Impatiently, Lucy dove into the water of Lake Eden.

It was bracingly cold. She felt the breath catch in her throat as the shock of the cold made her heart jump. She swam out a ways, floated on her back, and swam back into shore.

By the time she arrived, Cecil was standing ankle deep in the water, his shoes and socks discarded, and his pants rolled up past his calves.

"That's your limit?" Lucy asked, disappointed.

"I'm afraid I am not a Haimowitz," Cecil said. "You bohemian kids."

Lucy went to Cecil and took his hands in hers. "Oh, Cecil Weiss," she said. "Don't you see? Life is short and more tenuous than it has ever been since 1918. We need to live it while we still

84

can."

In response, Cecil got down on his knees, in the water, getting his trousers wet.

Uh-oh, Lucy thought. On the one hand, she was impressed that Cecil had the gumption to get his pants wet. On the other hand, OMG, what was he about to do?

Cecil produced a small box, which he opened. It contained a ring.

"Lucy Haimowitz, will you consent to be my wife?" he said.

OMG, Lucy thought. What am I going to do say?

Not knowing how to tactfully say no, Lucy said yes.

She didn't really want to marry Cecil. But she didn't want to lose him, either. And she knew if she said no, she'd lose him. In addition, they were quarantined together, so how the hell was that supposed to work if she turned him down? She could just imagine him sulking around the house, refusing to speak to her.

So, she said yes.

Cecil rose to his feet, and Lucy tried to kiss him, pulling his surgical mask off his mouth.

Cecil pulled away, and held his surgical mask securely on his face. "We really shouldn't," he said. "Not until it's safe. Social distancing and all that."

Lucy thought to herself this was really going to be a challenge, being married to this guy.

Just then, she heard a splash, and turned around to see Freddy, naked as she, emerge from the lake.

"Hello, Lucy and Cecil," Freddy cried. "Lucy, I see your sunburn has faded but your ass has gotten quite a bit bigger since we quarantined."

Lucy scowled at her brother. "Hello, Freddy," she said. "I see your penis has gotten quite a bit smaller."

"That's not fair," Freddy said. "The water is still freezing from the spring run-off."

Lucy scrutinized Freddy's unsuccessful attempt at a "quarantine beard," which made him look as if he were wearing a perpetual, uneven five-o'clock shadow.

Minnie emerged from the water just then, also naked, her pale body ruddy from the cold water. "Hi, Lucy!" she called. "Hi Cecil!"

Lucy turned to look at her. God, she thought, what wouldn't she give for a nineteen-year-old body. And she was only twenty-three. Of course Minnie – and Freddy for that matter – had no idea how lucky they were. Youth is wasted on the young.

Then Lucy thought how self-indulgent she was being to think of herself as anything other than young. She was wasting her youth by thinking this way.

This made her feel guilty. Then she thought she was wasting her youth by feeling guilty. If she wasted her energy thinking like this at twenty-three, how would she feel when she was thirty? Forty? Fifty?

How would she feel being married to Cecil at those ages?

She physically shuddered at the thought.

"Are you cold, Lucy?" Cecil asked.

Lucy ignored Cecil.

"Hi, Minnie," Lucy said, pleasantly, snapping out of it. "I'm glad you're enjoying Lake Eden."

Then George rose from the water and stood ankle deep, also as naked as his companions.

Lucy gasped. Even with the effect upon him of the cold of the spring run-off, George was a satisfying sight to see on this balmy spring day. He looked quite radiant, she thought. Unlike her brother, his quarantine beard was coming in quite nicely, and made him look just a little bit Viking-ish, in the best possible way.

She looked at her now-fiancé, briefly, and noticed, not for the first time, that Cecil, ever the man of steady habits, remained clean-shaven even in quarantine, but for the trim mustache he kept perched above his upper lip like a skinny caterpillar at rest.

Lucy turned back to George.

"Hi George," Lucy said, somewhat breathlessly.

"Hi, Lucy," George said. "You're looking well."

What did he mean by that? Lucy wondered. Did he mean she was looking good? Should she be flattered? Offended?

"We have to stop meeting like this," Lucy said, immediately regretting it.

She had not told Cecil about the sandbar, nor had she intended to.

George looked perplexed. "Why must we?" he asked.

Cecil, thankfully, appeared uninterested and oblivious to the subtext of the conversation, and did not seem curious as to why this was not the first such meeting for George and Lucy.

Quite suddenly, Minnie and Freddy ran past her, and up the path.

Freddy was showing her the rope swing, Lucy thought.

She watched them run up the path. God, the thought, she would kill for a tushie like Minnie's.

She looked at George and Cecil, and wondered, if it came to it, which one would she kill for a tushie like Minnie's?

She immediately settled on Cecil.

Lucy recognized there was something amiss in her choosing a man whom she barely knew and had once kissed naked upon a sandbar over her own fiancé, but she chose not to dwell on it. She was not, after all, going to kill anyone over Minnie's tushie. She would have to be satisfied with her own.

A joyful cry diverted her attention, and she looked about thirty feet away to see Freddy appearing out of the trees, swinging high up above the water on the end of the thick rope. He relinquished his grip upon the rope at the highest point, seemed to hover for a moment, then plunged into the water.

Minnie shrieked with delight. A moment later she too appeared above the water swinging at the end of the rope, then she too released her grip, her pale, ruddy flesh framed for a moment against the bright blue sky, and then she too plunged into the water beside Freddy.

They swam back to George and Lucy, ran back up the path, and repeated the process.

As Minnie and Freddy continued to swing on the rope, drop into the water, swim back to the shore, run up the pathway, and do the whole thing all over again, Lucy asked George, "how is your father's memoir going?"

"Oh, good God, that's all the world needs," Cecil grumbled. "Another memoir."

George and Lucy ignored him, both.

"It's going quite well, thanks for asking," George said. "Dad has a lot to write about."

Just then, Lucy heard the sound of rustling on the path. Someone was coming this way.

A moment later, her mother, Izzy Emison, Charlotte, and Rabbi Bobe appeared on the path, each wearing a face mask.

Izzy and the Rabbi's quarantine beards were both sprouting admirably, Lucy thought.

Neither George nor Lucy attempted to hide their nakedness, but Cecil did run onto the shore and quickly tried to put on his socks and shoes.

Freddy and Minnie were running part way up the path on one of their circuits at that moment. Minnie turned around and waved.

"Hi Dad!" Minnie called, brightly.

Then she turned away and continued to run up the path until, moments later, Freddy and Minnie again appeared, one after the other, on the rope swing. After both plunged back into Lake Eden, they swam again back to rejoin George and Lucy.

The four of them stood ankle deep in the water, casually looking at their elders . . . plus Charlotte and Cecil . . . standing on the shore.

The Rabbi very uncomfortably attempted not to look at his naked daughter, while also attempting not to look away too sharply and give her the impression he thought her nakedness was shameful. This left him in something of a loop, as his head pivoted awkwardly back and forth, failing to settle anywhere comfortably.

Mrs. Haimowitz was less equivocal. "Oh, Freddy and Lucy, really, must you force all your friends to join you in your savagery?"

Charlotte's eyes, after momentarily widening in shock, were now both closed tight.

Izzy, on the other hand, heartily approved. "Young people enjoying the nature God has given them!" he shouted. "As it should be! Mistrust any enterprise that requires the wearing of clothes, I always say! Carry on!"

"Lotte!" Freddy called. "You should join us!"

"Yes, Charlotte," Izzy agreed. "Leave us old people and embrace your youth!"

"I'm just fine as I am, thanks," Charlotte said quietly, her voice choked, her eyes still closed tightly.

"I have something of an announcement to make," Cecil said.

Oh, no, Cecil, thought Lucy. Not now.

"Lucy Haimowitz has consented to be my wife," Cecil said.

This announcement was met with a moment of thundering silence.

Lucy felt an odd sensation in her gut that she thought might have be the sensation one feels when one's soul drops out of one's body. She suddenly felt more truly naked than she had ever in her life.

Cecil appeared offended. "I'm sorry if the news doesn't meet with your approval," he said, peevishly.

"Nonsense!" Mrs. Haimowitz cried brightly, deftly saving the day. "Cecil! Mazel Tov, you two!"

Her mother kissed Cecil, although Cecil did not remove his facemask when she did, and the Rabbi and Mr. Emison rubbed elbows with him in lieu of shaking hands. Neither man appeared overjoyed, but they made a show of expressing their satisfaction at the turn of events.

Minnie ran through the water and took Lucy in a bright, tight embrace.

"I am so happy for you!" Minnie shouted.

Lucy felt a bit odd enveloped in the arms of this girl she had only recently begun to get to know, but she accepted the embrace, and returned it.

Freddy glowered at her disapprovingly.

George only looked at her with an expression more of concern than disappointment, Lucy thought. Lucy was disappointed George didn't appear more disappointed, and concerned that he appeared so concerned.

Lucy's mother came to the edge of the water, but did not venture in. "You two will make each other very happy, dear," she said.

And then Lucy noticed something surprising.

Charlotte was taking off her sneakers and socks. Then she rolled up the cuffs of her pants.

Barefoot, Charlotte waded into the water, right up to Lucy.

She looked deeply into Lucy's eyes. Lucy could not read the emotion within them.

Then Charlotte enveloped her cousin in a tight embrace.

"I am so happy for you, Lulu," she whispered. "I am so happy for you."

Lucy, recognizing what an effort it must have taken Charlotte to overcome her discomfort and embrace her like this, hugged her back, and thanked her.

Then Charlotte, her eyes moist, made her way back to shore, where she put back on her socks and sneakers.

"Well, we'll leave you young people to your fun," Lucy's mother said. "Tonight we will celebrate."

"I'll go with you," Cecil told Mrs. Haimowitz. "Lucy, I'll see you back at the house."

Awkwardly, the elders, with Charlotte and Cecil, made their way up the path and out of sight.

"Well," Freddy said after a moment. "I think it's time for a tick check, don't you?"

Freddy and Minnie dove into the water and swam across the lake, to where they had left their clothes.

George lingered.

He looked at Lucy.

Lucy looked at him.

"Well?" Lucy said. "Are you going to congratulate me?"

"You can't marry him," George blurted out.

"Excuse me?"

"You know you can't. He'll never make you happy."

"What do you know about anything?" Lucy said, her heart sinking with the anxiety that George might be right.

"He's not your type," George said.

"What do you know about my type?"

"I know that he isn't it."

"You don't know anything about me," Lucy protested.

"I bet I know more about you than he does," George said. "I know Egon Schiele's painting *The Family* reduced you to tears; I know your first instinct was to help a stranger infected with the virus instead of to turn away; I know you are unashamed of your nakedness and unafraid to embrace the natural world and all its natural beauty, in all of yours; I know you sing and play piano with an unaffected honesty that captivates your listeners; I know when you met a religious fanatic risking his life to hang from a crucifix in a rainstorm, you talked him down; I know when you met a gas station attendant who lacked the courage to move forward with his life, you gave him that courage; and I know you weren't afraid to follow your heart and kiss me on that sandbar."

"We've just met!" Lucy cried. "We're barely more than strangers."

"I wiped the snot from your face. Has Cecil ever done that? Do you think he ever would?"

Lucy couldn't stand to hear George talk anymore, so she marched up to him, put her arms around him, and kissed him. George rolled with it, and took her in his arms, and kissed her back.

They kissed for longer this time, and their hands began caressing one another intimately. Lucy's heart raced and her breath was short. She felt she could disappear into that kiss, that embrace, those caresses.

She felt George's loins begin to harden against her, and she pulled away.

"I'm sorry," she said. "I am so sorry."

"Don't be sorry," George said. He stood there, making no attempt to hide his erection, which Lucy tried and failed not to look at.

"I have to go now," she said, climbing to the shore and gathering up her clothes. "You have to go now. Why do you have to confuse me like this?"

"You're not confused," George said. "You know exactly what you feel. You just won't allow yourself to feel it."

"Don't be so Goddamn sure of yourself, George!" Lucy said. "I'm not a child. Don't treat me like one. Don't assume you understand me better than I understand myself."

"I don't think that," George said. "But I do think I trust you better than you trust yourself."

Lucy didn't know what to say to that, so she held her clothes and sneakers in a bundle and ran naked down the path towards home, leaving George standing alone in the water with his tumescence slowly diminishing.

She waited until the lake was out of sight before she stopped and struggled back into her clothes. She was crying and she didn't know why. Dressed, she laced up her sneakers and ran for home, using the bandana that served as her facemask to wipe away her tears and snot, wishing George was there to do it for her.

That night they contacted everyone they knew via Zoom, Skype, Facetime, and Google Meets, and celebrated the engagement in the backyard with bottles of really nice wine from the cellar, and a sumptuous feast of kosher grilled meat prepared by Rabbi Bobe. Lucy felt events were spinning out of her control; now, everyone she had ever known knew about her engagement to Cecil Weiss, and she had just kissed George for the second time while both of them were naked. And she couldn't stop thinking about his erection, and the way it had felt pressed against her.

It was all so confusing.

When at last they contacted the Miss Alans, they found only Catherine.

"I'm afraid Teresa is in hospital," Catherine said. "She has the virus."

"Oh, no," Lucy said, feeling her heart sink. "That's terrible."

"Half our congregation does," Catherine said. "You were right, Freddy."

"I hope the Reverend has realized the error of his ways," Freddy said.

"I don't know," Catherine said. "He's in hospital as well, sick with the virus. They won't allow anyone to visit either one of them."

Lucy was upset beyond measure. She went downstairs to her father's old music room. Her dad, a highly successful lawyer, had also been a passionate collector of music on vinyl. After he died, she had come down here often to remember him by playing his old records.

She found the Beatles *Abbey Road*, still alphabetized, and flipped it to side two. She put the needle on the record.

"Here Comes the Sun" made her feel more hopeful, as it always did, but it was the sixteen-minute melody from "You Never Give Me Your Money" through "The End" that she really allowed herself to get lost in.

She stood in front of the turntable, taking the music's textures, the lyric's imagery of girls in bathroom windows, the singing of lullabies, the carrying of weight, of the love you give and the love you take.

Afterwards, she patiently waited the fourteen seconds until "Her Majesty" came on, its interrupted twenty-three seconds bringing the album to a close.

"My mom used to listen to that record," she heard George say.

He was standing by the stairs.

"How old were you when your mom passed?" Lucy said.

"I was fourteen."

"I was fourteen when I lost my dad," Lucy said. "He had a heart attack. I heard your mom had cancer."

"She was in a lot of pain. She asked Dad and me to mix her a cocktail of drugs. I'm not sure what was in it. The doctor had given her and Dad instructions for when things got really bad, even though he wasn't supposed to. We crushed up the pills and mixed them in a glass as we sat by her as she drank it and just faded away."

The information left Lucy momentarily speechless, and filled with sympathy for George.

It was also clear to her why Reverend Eager had accused him of murder. It was even more clear to her that Reverend Eager was a complete dick. She hoped the Reverend died of the virus. Then she felt guilty about hoping that, so she hoped it back.

"I'm so sorry for your loss," Lucy said, although she thought that sounded lame.

"I'm sorry for yours," George said.

"It still hurts, right?" Lucy said. "It does for me."

"It never goes away. You just get more used to it," George said.

Lucy was torn between two powerful, competing desires: to kiss George again, and to burst into tears.

The air between them was thick with anticipation.

Lucy pointed to the upright piano against the wall. "You play? I know you sing Ok."

"I play ukulele a bit," George said.

"Do you really?" Lucy said, taking Freddy's ukulele from atop the piano and handing it to George. "Prove it."

"Uh-oh," George said.

Lucy sat at the piano and played the opening chords to "Hey Jude."

"Can you manage that?' Lucy asked.

George plucked a few strings. "I think I can keep up," he said.

They played and sang the song together, and Lucy felt her spirits soar. Her confusions did not dissipate, but they no longer vexed her so, at least while they played.

They were right in the middle of what Lucy thought had to be the best piano/ukulele chorus of "na na na na-na-na-na" when Cecil suddenly appeared on the stairs.

The sight of him there wearing his face mask infuriated Lucy.

"Oh, there you are," Cecil said, not even having the decency to wait until they finished. "I was sent to find you."

"We're playing the Beatles," Lucy said, without stopping, going right back into the chorus.

"Well, don't keep everyone waiting," Cecil said.

Lucy answered with another "na-na" chorus.

"I never much liked the Beatles," Cecil said, as he started back up the stairs. "They're rather over-rated."

For the third time that day, Lucy considered killing Cecil Weiss.

A few days later Lucy's work announced a special on-line event: Eleanor Lavin was going to preview some passages for her novel-in-progress.

Lucy worked hard the next few days on the social media campaign to build an audience for the event. When the night finally came, the Ms. Alans both joined remotely, Catherine from home and Teresa from the hospital.

Lucy joined with her mother, Freddy, Minnie, Cecil, Charlotte, and George in her living room to watch the event, streaming on their big screen smart TV. Cecil wore his mask. The others did not. The Rabbi and Mr. Emison, she hoped, were watching the event from their respective homes.

Ms. Lavin read passages from her book about two young people, Leonora and Tony, who meet at a beach hotel when they swap rooms so Leonora can have a view of the ocean.

Hmm, Lucy thought. That's an interesting coincidence.

Later, they meet at a museum, where Leonora is overcome by the emotional impact of the artwork, and Tony offers her a tissue.

Still later, Leonora is standing naked on a sandbar at a clothing optional beach, when Tom climbs up to join her.

"'Leonora,'" Ms. Lavin read, with feeling, "'stood pensive and alone in her nakedness. Before her lay the rich community of the beach, dotted over with many a smiling sunbather, each clothed only with the sun. The season was spring.'"

Uh-oh, Lucy thought.

"'Behind her, a golden haze lay over the ocean,'" she read. "'Afar torsos of porpoises undulated upon the surface, while the sandbar upon which she stood was lapped by gentle waves at her ankles. Unobserved, Tony, as naked as she, climbed upon the sandbar behind her—'"

Lest Cecil should see her face she turned to George and saw his face.

Ms. Lavin read: "'There came from his lips no wordy protestation such as formal lovers use. No eloquence was his, nor did he suffer from the lack of it. He simply placed a garland of bluebonnets around her neck and enfolded her in his manly arms, their bare flesh to flesh, and he kissed her with abandon.'"

George did not look at her, but Lucy knew he knew.

Lucy's mother had high praise for the event at its conclusion. Cecil, blissfully unaware of the source material, criticized Ms. Lavin's "turgid prose." George slinked off somewhere. Freddy and Minnie congratulated Lucy for her hard work, then went out to the back yard to play badminton. Charlotte looked pale and forlorn.

Pulling her cousin aside, Lucy said, "Lotte, how much did you tell Ms. Lavin?"

"Lulu, I am so sorry," Charlotte said.

"I didn't realize the two of you had become such confidants."

"We have become Facebook friends," Charlotte admitted. "I will unfriend her immediately."

"A little late for that, don't you think?"

Cecil continued to prattle on about how bad Ms. Lavin's writing was, so as soon as she was able, Lucy snuck downstairs to the music room and went to the piano. She lifted the fallboard and saw an index card that had been placed upon the keys. She lifted the index card and examined it.

Upon it, a question mark had been drawn in crayon.

The next day, as Lucy and Cecil hiked the trail to Lake Eden, Cecil with his mask on, Lucy with her bandana around her neck, at the ready in case they encountered fellow hikers, Lucy said, "Cecil, we can't get married."

Cecil, who evidently thought she was joking, said, "and why can't we get married?"

"Because I don't love you, Cecil," Lucy said.

Cecil's conviction that this was all a joke was beginning to weaken. "Why don't you love me anymore?" he asked, a plaintive note in his voice.

"It's not a question of 'anymore,'" Lucy explained. "It's more a question of 'never did.'"

This stopped Cecil in his tracks. He looked at her, his eyes bereft, even if the rest of his face remained masked. "Is this because I won't kiss you?" he asked.

"It's not the kissing," Lucy said, "so much as it is the living."

"I don't understand."

"Cecil, you're no fun."

"That's not true," Cecil complained. "I'm really quite a lot of fun."

"Fun for you is mocking Eleanor Lavin's prose."

"She's a terrible writer."

"Even so, you don't need to make fun of everything. She's a friend and a colleague. The gears of wibbly-wobbly spacetime won't grind to a halt if you stop taking every opportunity to make fun of things."

"'Wibbly-wobbly spacetime?'" Cecil repeated.

"It's a *Doctor Who* allusion," Lucy explained.

"Oh," Cecil said. "I've never watched."

"Of course you haven't."

"I didn't know you felt that way about *Doctor Who* or Ms. Lavin," Cecil said.

"It's not just Ms. Lavin," Lucy insisted. "Or *Doctor Who*. What do you like? What do you enjoy? What do you find fun? Nothing at all. You don't like music."

"I like music."

"You don't like the Beatles."

"The Beatles are over-rated."

"Your sense of your own impeccable taste is over-rated."

"That was cruel," said Cecil.

"Sometimes we have to be cruel to be kind. Which song is that?"

"Which song is what?"

"Never mind," Lucy said, knowing full Cecil had probably never even heard of Nick Lowe.

"Most music critics agree with me about the Beatles, you know," Cecil said.

"See, that's exactly what I'm talking about," Lucy said, certain now more than ever of the correctness of the course she was taking. "That's absolutely not true. But you think it's true because truth for you is what validates your prejudices, not what is objectively true."

"In terms of what is objectively true, I've been a lot more careful to behave according to scientific recommendations during this pandemic than anyone else in your household."

"Yes, but you use your masking and social distancing as an excuse for your emotional remoteness," Lucy said. "You're not really into personal affection even when there is no virus."

Cecil was thoughtful. "That's true. Bodies are so . . . clumsy. Inelegant. We kiss with the same orifice with which we eat, spit, cough, vomit, and sneeze."

"Through which we also laugh, sing, sigh, and express ourselves, Cecil," Lucy said. "But you don't like kissing, hugging, swimming, singing, or snogging. You only want to make love with the lights off, and you don't really enjoy making love all that much. You treat it like a not entirely unpleasant obligation. Lie back and think of England and all that except that we're not English, you're the one lying on your back, and you're probably thinking of Heidegger. And you've managed to avoid any intimacy whatsoever since the Stay at Home order."

"Only as a precaution."

"No. Not only as a precaution. Because you don't really enjoy it."

Cecil considered. "You're right, Lucy," he said. "I see that now. Only . . . I still do love you."

Lucy took a moment before she replied. "Be that as it may, Cecil," she said, "I cannot live life with someone who cannot enjoy life."

"I enjoy life."

"But the things you enjoy in life, Cecil," Lucy said, "are things you enjoy just as much without me."

They were approaching Lake Eden now, and as they grew nearer, the sound of plunking ukuleles and lilting voices grew louder.

They found Freddy and Minnie standing ankle deep in the

water, playing ukulele and singing "All Together Now" by the Beatles. That they were both naked but for the ukuleles they played, Lucy found both unsurprising and oddly ordinary. Just another day at Lake Eden during the pandemic.

Unnoticed, Cecil and Lucy watched and listened for a while.

When Freddy and Minnie finished, Lucy applauded enthusiastically, Cecil rather less so.

"Come and join us!" Minnie called.

Lucy demurred.

"I think," Cecil said, "that were I not here with you, you would join them."

"If I had my ukulele, I probably would," Lucy admitted. "Even if you *were* here with me."

"And I would never, under any circumstances," Cecil said, sadly. "Even if I knew how to play ukulele. I think I do understand, Lucy. I really do. I do not approve of, appreciate, or enjoy the things you like to do. I hate to say this, but − I could never make you happy. You would always feel constrained by me. I don't want to constrain you. I want to make you happy. I think the best thing I can do to make you happy is to agree with you. You should not marry me. You will not be happy. And that, my dear Lucy, I do not think I could stand, for you to be unhappy."

For the first time in a long time, Lucy felt genuine affection welling up inside her for Cecil Weiss. She was surprised and delighted by the equanimity he displayed.

It was not enough to make her love him. But she definitely did not want to kill him any longer.

The next few weeks, things got even weirder.

Wearing a mask became political, with conservatives refusing on the grounds it violated their freedom, and liberals accepting the mask as a sensible measure in the interest of public health.

Armed protestors who refused to wear masks or to social distance besieged state capitols, shutting down legislative sessions, protesting stay-at-home orders, insisting that hairdressers and restaurant workers be forced to risk their lives in order not to inconvenience those who preferred to brandish weapons instead of facemasks.

Over Memorial Day weekend, young people all over the

country were reported recreating in crowded conditions without masks on.

Reports circulated of the imminent arrival of "murder hornets," aggressive, giant hornets who destroyed bee colonies.

The CDC warned of aggressive, starving "cannibal rats," desperate due to the lack of food waste from restaurants, all closed down due to the pandemic shutdown.

The Air Force released videos of UFOs.

Reports began to circulate that the Yellowstone "super volcano" was showing signs of waking up.

States around the country were beginning the process of reopening, many without taking appropriate measures to prevent a second wave of viral infections, or even to have fully brought the first wave under control.

Meanwhile, the nation-wide death toll exceeded one hundred and sixteen thousand, more Americans than had died in the fighting during the First World War.

Cecil kept to his room most of the time, only briefly appearing for meals. Lucy implored him not to travel back to his own place, during the virus pandemic, and risk exposure on the train.

Freddy and Minnie spent more and more time in each other's company, playing badminton and ukulele, hiking and swimming.

George continued to assist his father on his memoir and writing commentary for his online socialist journal.

Rabbi Bobe conducted a full program of virtual, on-line services.

Mother continued to do a lot of gardening.

Charlotte started quietly biting her nails all the time.

Lucy was spending more and more time alone, and she was enjoying her time alone. She was self-aware enough to recognize she found George attractive; but after extricating herself from her Cecil-entanglement, she found she did not want to investigate the George Question, as she had come to think of it, associating her interest in the young Mr. Emison with the crayon-drawings of question marks George had left for her.

She read books: *A Room with a View*, *The Plot Against America*, and *The Searchers*. She found *A Room with a View* absolutely charming;

she found *The Plot Against America* absolutely chilling, and frighteningly plausible; she found *The Searchers* thrilling and racially problematical.

She began to watch submarine movies. It took her a while to realize she probably identified with people contained in small spaces with the same people day after day. She found movies about disasters on Soviet and Russian submarines particularly compelling. *Kursk* and *K-9: The Widowmaker* she found especially effective. There was something about the efforts of the characters in these movies to pull together and save lives while their political leadership completely abandoned them with utterly depraved indifference and disregard that felt like a metaphor for America during the pandemic.

After that she moved onto movies set on trains, another enclosed space in which human dramas and comedies played out. She watched *The Cassandra Complex,* about a deadly virus outbreak on a passenger train. The movie, which had a rather grim ending, hit a little too close to home. It did, however, lead to a deep dive into 1970s disaster movies.

The Towering Inferno was easily the best, with central performances by Paul Newman and Steve McQueen, in their only film together, that simply could not be beat. Lucy found a subplot with an aging Fred Astaire as an incompetent con-man to be particularly poignant. *The Poseidon Adventure* was a close second, although Lucy found Gene Hackman's performance a bit too yell-y. Special mention went to *Juggernaut,* directed by Richard Lester, who had also directed *A Hard Day's Night, Help!, How I Won the War, The Three Musketeers, The Four Musketeers,* and *Robin and Marian.* While not the best on the "disaster-y" elements, it easily surpassed the others in terms of the minutiae of characterization among the passengers and crew on a British cruise ship.

Lucy also decided that Richard Harris was the best actor with the worst haircuts of the 1970s.

Things began to unravel beyond Summer Street.

A black jogger was murdered by armed citizens. A black front-line health care worker was murdered by cops while she slept in her bed. A black citizen was murdered by a cop who pressed his knee into the back of the man's neck until he asphyxiated.

Protests broke out across the country. Most of the protestors wore masks. Many did not socially distance. Cops fired tear gas and rubber bullets to try to disperse them. Cops arrested a CNN news team covering a protest in Minneapolis. In Kentucky, cops fired pepper balls directly at a news crew covering protests there.

Rioting, arson, and looting erupted around the country. Right-wing politicians blamed the protestors. Video appeared of suspicious characters, mostly white men, committing vandalism while protestors tried to stop them. Rumors began to circulate of "agent provocateurs," possibly white supremacists, possibly working for foreign powers, possibly both, trying to provoke violence in the hope of either sparking a civil war or assisting the president's reelection campaign, or both. The Attorney General accused Antifa of being behind the violence, but did not produce any evidence. The president accused a seventy-five-year-old man who had been brutalized by police of being Antifa, but everyone knew it was a lie.

Journalists were repeatedly arrested or assaulted by police.

The president ordered Federal forces to clear peaceful protestors from Lafayette Park with tear gas, pepper balls, rubber bullets, and swinging batons, assaulting an Australian news crew in the process, so the president could walk across the park and stand in front of a church holding a bible for a photo op.

The New Yorker reported that the president had ordered the Chairman of the Joint Chiefs of Staff to send in military troops to occupy major American cities to put down the protests, but the Chairman had angrily refused, getting into a shouting match with his own Commander-in-Chief.

Lucy wondered if America had not been on the brink of dictatorship . . . and if the country had really pulled back from the brink.

In early June, the Summer Street Quarantine Bubble participated in a local "March for Justice Against Racist State Violence." Cecil and Charlotte stayed behind, each alone in their separate rooms. About two hundred people showed up, more than Lucy had seen in one place since the Stay at Home order was issued. Everyone wore masks and marched six feet apart to maintain social distancing. Police observed cautiously from the sidelines.

When everyone returned home from the march, making sure to wash hands and dispose of masks, Lucy found an email from Catherine Alan, who informed her she would soon be joining the rest of them on Summer Street, where she had purchased a small cottage, locally known as Forster Villa, right next to the Emison home.

Oh, good, Lucy thought. Our Quarantine Bubble can expand.

The email went on to regretfully inform Lucy that both Teresa Alan and Reverend Eager had died in hospital due to complications from the virus.

Oh, no, Lucy thought.

Lucy quickly wrote Catherine Alan a note expressing her sorrow and condolence and welcoming her to Summer Street. Then she grabbed a fresh mask and left the house.

Lucy went for a hike, her feelings roiling inside of her confusedly. She had expected to be seized with howling sobs of despair. Instead, she felt benumbed. She felt spiritually hollow. She felt emotionally empty.

She also felt very guilty for previously wishing that the Reverend die of the virus, and she hoped she had taken that back at the time with sufficient conviction so his death was not the result of her wishes.

She walked along the hiking path, taking in the smell of the dirt, of the leaves and wildflowers, of the gentle breezes of late Spring.

The Haimowitzs, the Emisons, the Bobes, they were lucky, she thought. They had homes in which to stay at home. They had jobs they could do from home. They had so far avoided the virus. They did not have to fear for their lives from police who did not pull guns on them on a regular basis, as happened to people who weren't lucky enough to live on Summer Street and did not carry with them the protective shield of white privilege.

The world was a disaster movie, but the pacing of it was excruciatingly slow. When the end of the world as they knew it finally came, would they even know it? Did Rome know when it had fallen?

Lucy came to Lake Eden and, to her tremendous surprise, she

saw Cecil and Charlotte, standing knee-deep in the water, looking dreamily into one another's eyes.

They wore face masks, gloves on their hands . . . and nothing else, other than Cecil's glasses.

They held one another's gloved hands tenderly.

Lucy was flabbergasted. Out of all the unexpected things she had never expected this had been the absolute least expected. She could fathom that Charlotte and Cecil had somehow found each other, Charlotte in her loneliness, and Cecil in his heartbreak – if she could flatter herself that what Cecil was feeling after she dumped him was, indeed, heartbreak. What she could not fathom was that either of them would bathe in Lake Eden in their nakedness, much less together – it was so utterly out of character for both of them.

Lucy wondered if, somehow, finding one another had mysteriously sparked a new joyfulness and sense of adventure inside of themselves, the manifestation of which she was now witness. She wondered if both Charlotte and Cecil might have hidden depths of strangeness, if not of meaning, within them that she had never suspected.

Lucy and Cecil turned to her, and immediately stopped holding hands. They stood there awkwardly, and, to the degree Lucy could discern as much behind their face masks, looked aghast, and guilty.

"This isn't what it looks like," Charlotte mumbled behind her mask.

"What is it, then?" Lucy asked.

Charlotte and Cecil exchanged a glance.

"What do *you* think it is?" Cecil asked.

"I think the two of you have fallen in love," Lucy said.

Charlotte and Cecil exchanged another glance.

"Then it is actually what it looks like," Charlotte admitted.

Charlotte sat down on a rock that protruded from the water.

Then Charlotte screamed.

It was, Lucy thought, perhaps the most blood-curdling scream she had ever heard.

"I've been stabbed in the ass by a murder hornet!" Charlotte cried and, quite crazed and quite naked but for her gloves and facemask, ran past Lucy and down the path, screaming all the way.

Instinctively, Lucy ran after her.

Charlotte had made it all the way to Summer Street, past startled hikers, and was running naked through the residential neighborhood, screaming all the way, attracting the astonished attention of her neighbors, before Lucy caught up to her. She had to literally tackle her cousin around the midriff and bring her face-down on a neighbor's lawn.

Charlotte continued to struggle and scream, so Lucy sat upon her torso to pin her down and examine her posterior.

Charlotte had indeed been stabbed by a stinging insect; but it was not a murder hornet. It was just a regular bee. Crushed, it remained attached to Charlotte's tushie by its stinger, still deeply inserted into her flesh.

"Charlotte, be still!" Lucy commanded.

Charlotte froze, but continued to scream.

Gently, Lucy pinched the bee between her thumb and forefinger and slid the stinger out.

Charlotte continued to scream.

Lucy rolled off of her cousin. "Does it still hurt?" she asked.

Charlotte stopped screaming, and assessed her pain. "Not as much," she admitted. "But it hurt so much."

"Are you allergic to bee-stings?" Lucy asked.

"No," Charlotte said, "but I'm not sure about murder hornets."

"It was not a murder hornet," Lucy said. "It was a honey-bee."

"But it felt like an iron spike tipped with poisonous lava had been driven through my ass."

"That's what a bee sting on your ass is supposed to feel like," Lucy said.

As Charlotte rose, she noticed a small crowd of mostly masked individuals from the neighborhood had gathered around her. Her eyes widened as her embarrassment bloomed.

"I am so sorry," she whispered.

"Are you all right, dear?" said Ms. Blandings, who lived a few houses away from the Haimowitzs.

Charlotte was too mortified to answer.

Cecil appeared then. He had managed to pull his pants on, and stood bare-chested, with both his and Charlotte's clothing and sneakers in a bundle under his arm, his glasses, gloves, and mask sill in place.

"Charlotte," he said, his voice full of concern. "Are you Ok?"

Lucy discovered she was not at all upset that Cecil had so quickly found a replacement for her. If she was honest about it, she had to admit that Charlotte and Cecil made a much better fit.

When at length they returned to the Windy Corners, Cecil and Charlotte retired to her room to tend her wound, and Lucy went to the backyard, where she found George, Minnie, and Freddy singing "Here Comes the Sun" by George Harrison, accompanying themselves on ukulele.

"Lucy!" Freddy called when he saw her. "Join us!"

They had a ukulele set aside for her. Lucy grabbed it and joined them in time for the chorus.

As dusk began to fall, the fireflies appeared, their green glowing twinkle sparkling all around them.

That night, cable television was filled with images of violence and fires breaking out in cities all over the country. Police and protesters clashed. The president made threats about unleashing dogs and "ominous weapons," and reveled in the possibility that protesters would be hurt "really bad."

Lucy felt more than ever that everything was going to shit.

She almost missed a small but heartbreaking news item that flashed across the crawl on the bottom of the screen:

Paul "Bear" Vasquez, the man responsible for the viral "double rainbow" video that Jimmy Fallon had turned into a mock-Neil Young song and which George and Lucy had sung together in the van on the way to pick up Freddy, had died, a victim of the virus.

The next day, Lucy went out into the backyard with her ukulele and, thinking herself alone, played and sang "Hell You Talmbout," by Janelle Monáe and the Wondaland Artist Collective, that recited the names of black Americans murdered by racist violence.

Towards the end of the song, she added new names: George Floyd, Ahmaud Arbery, and Breonna Taylor.

She finished the song and stood there for a time, quiet, feeling a lump in her gut.

She felt it was presumptuous of a privileged white girl to sing this song. Presumptuous and useless. She had to find ways to better use her privilege to help enact real change.

"I came over to bring you this," she heard George say.

She looked and saw him there, holding a massive stack of paper in his hand.

"What is that?" Lucy asked. "Is that your dad's memoir?"

"It is," George said. "We both agreed, we'd like you to be the first to read it."

Lucy took the manuscript. It was heavy. "Why me?" she said.

"Because," George said, "we thought you would appreciate it."

Lucy clutched the manuscript to her chest. "Thank you. I'm honored."

George smiled. "Read it first. Then tell us if you're still honored."

"I'll still be honored," Lucy said.

"But give us your honest feedback," George said. "We respect your opinion."

Lucy was baffled. "Why?"

George looked at her as if the question was baffling. "Because you feel things, deeply, Lucy. Because you understand things that others don't even know exist."

"I don't think I really do," Lucy said.

"I think you do," George said. "That's why I'm so much in love with you."

Well, Lucy thought. That certainly raised the stakes. "George," she said, "there's so much going on."

"I know," George agreed. "But in the end, what has anyone really got to get through it all, except each other?"

It was a good question, and Lucy didn't think she had a better answer.

"I feel like I'd like to kiss you now," Lucy said. "But if I do, I don't know what will happen."

"It won't be our first kiss," George said.

"But it could be the last," Lucy said. "Or the first of many more. I really don't know. I feel like it's either going to be the end . . . or the beginning."

"Do you want to find out?" George asked, quietly.

"I don't know," Lucy said. "Do you?"

George waited to answer.

"I think I do, yes," he said.

Lucy hesitated.

"There's so much that's screwed up in the world right now," she said. "Doesn't it freak you out?"

"It does," George admitted.

"How can we just go on like everything's normal?"

"Nothing's normal," George said. "But that doesn't mean we can't go on. I mean, if you think about it, that means we have to go on. We have no choice. We have to get up every day and we have to fight. We have to struggle. We can't stay on the sidelines. We have to protest, and organize, and vote, and advocate. We have to do our part to make things better. We have to be better. We have to be better allies, better citizens, better people. We have to defund and abolish the police. We have to be anti-racist. We have to be pro-love. To do otherwise is to give into despair, which is what the fascist oligarchy wants."

"'What day is it?' said Pooh," Lucy said, quoting a meme. "'The day we burn this fascist oligarchy to the ground,' said Piglet. 'My favorite day,' said Pooh."

George smiled. "Exactly."

"You must go on. I can't go on. I'll go on," Lucy said.

"Samuel Beckett was right about that," George said.

Lucy found it sexy that George knew his Beckett, and so she went to him and kissed him.

She wrapped her arms around him and he wrapped his around hers and they put their mouths together and they kissed, and she felt her heart race, and she felt her heart find its home as their lips and their tongues found each other.

And after, George said, "What do you think? The first, or the last?"

In reply, Lucy kissed him again.

The End.

ABOUT THE AUTHOR

Peter Ullian is the author *The Last Electric House* (Swamp Angel Press); *The Fevered Dream-Crimes of Pulp-Fiction Poets and Other Love Stories: New and Selected Poems* (Lion Autumn Music Publishing); *Secret Histories and Exobiologies: Poems* (The Poet's Haven); *Pan-American* (NoPassport Press); *New American Century and Fair City: Two Plays* (NoPassport Press); *Valhalla Correctional* (Smith & Kraus); *The Triumphant Return of Blackbird Flynt* (Broadway Play Publishing); and *Big Bossman* (Broadway Play Publishing). His work for the stage has been produced off-Broadway, at regional theatres throughout the U.S.A, and internationally in England, Scotland, the Czech Republic, and South Africa. He is the 2019-2020 Poet Laureate for the City of Beacon, NY.

www.ingramcontent.com/pod-product-compliance
Lightning Source LLC
Chambersburg PA
CBHW030553130626
46552CB00006B/2529